She strode a

'Do you always
or am I an exce

The question halted Gaby in mid-stride, then
she hurried on, hoping Jack hadn't noticed.

'I didn't say I didn't want to take you,' she
replied.

'You didn't have to, lady. Since the moment
we met you've been sending out "stand clear
of me" signals that are so strong, they make
words superfluous.'

'Don't be ridiculous,' she argued, but the
words lacked the conviction they needed.

Having pursued many careers—from schoolteaching to pig farming—with varying degrees of success and plenty of enjoyment, **Meredith Webber** seized on the arrival of a computer in her house as an excuse to turn to what had always been a secret urge—writing. As she had more doctors and nurses in the family than any other professional people, the medical romance seemed the way to go! Meredith lives on the Gold Coast of Queensland, with her husband and teenage son.

FLIGHT INTO LOVE

BY
MEREDITH WEBBER

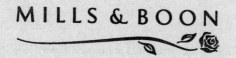

MILLS & BOON, the Rose Device and LOVE ON CALL
are trademarks of the publisher.
Harlequin Mills & Boon Limited,
Eton House, 18–24 Paradise Road, Richmond, Surrey TW9 1SR
This edition published by arrangement with
Harlequin Enterprises B.V.

© Meredith Webber 1995

ISBN 0 263 79338 9

Set in 10 on 12 pt Linotron Times
03-9509-53179

Typeset in Great Britain by CentraCet, Cambridge
Made and printed in Great Britain
Cover illustration by Simon Bishop

AUTHOR'S NOTE

WHILE Broome, Derby and Wyndham are very real towns, I have taken liberties with their airports and the Royal Flying Doctor Service base and staff, then populated the area with imaginary people. However, the Royal Flying Doctor Service—RFDS—is not only real, but is an incredible organisation which has made life in isolated regions like the Kimberleys safer and more secure for those who live beaneath its widespread wings. In 1992–93, the RFDS, Australia-wide, flew close to five million nautical miles, had contact with over one hundred and fifty thousand patients, transported over fourteen thousand ill or injured people, and made approximately forty thousand remote consultations by radio or telephone.

CHAPTER ONE

GABY circled the plane once again, squinting as the last fierce rays of the sun glinted off the fuselage. The feeling that something was wrong with it niggled deep in her bones.

'I've done a complete service, I've checked things that I usually only check after a thousand hours, I've tested every component. Jed Roberts flew her yesterday and didn't notice anything. She's OK, Gaby!' Fred Williams followed one step behind her, his wrinkled face screwed into even tighter lines as he listed the checks he'd made and frowned his disapproval.

'I suppose you're right, Fred,' she replied with an uncertain sigh, although her attention was still focused on the plane as if willing it to part with its secret ailment.

'Damn sure I'm right, young lady,' the mechanic said crisply. 'Now stop brooding over the thing, or I'll tell the boss you're going troppo and you'll be barred from flying.'

He patted her arm to soften the words and walked back toward the north-western hangar.

Gaby shuddered in reaction to the threat. Without her job, her life would be barren and empty, yet she couldn't still the tiny voice whispering deep within her. Something was wrong with Charlie Papa Bravo.

She circled it again, deliberately not thinking, hoping that the intuitive part of her brain might be able to dredge up something more than a vague premonitory doubt.

'This girl might know who to ask!' An American accent slurred the deep voice in a tantalising manner, so that the simple statement sounded like an enticement. Her footsteps slowed. Was she the 'girl' he meant? She wanted to think, not be polite to people who had no right to be out on the tarmac.

'I didn't think they had stewardesses on planes this small.'

She heard the second part of the conversation quite clearly. The man's companion was a woman—and a bitchy one at that, if her tone was anything to judge by! The 'stewardess' remark brought her out of her reverie, while the false assumption of what her smart uniform meant made the skin prickle to attention on the back of her neck.

Drawing herself up to her full five feet five, she came round the nose of the plane to confront the intruders. The wind that always seemed to blow at airports whipped ink-black hair across her face, and she lifted a hand to push it out of her eyes as she spoke to the strangers.

'Can I help you?'

It might have been a conventional courtesy but the words, coolly uttered, lacked any semblance of warmth or willingness to help.

'I shouldn't think so,' the female member of the couple replied in a voice even colder than the one Gaby had used. The man half smiled, and murmured something that Gaby suspected she was better off not hearing.

His blue eyes scanned from the top of her head to the tip of her toes with a tired, almost indifferent discernment that fed the little coils of anger already squirming beneath her skin.

'Just as well, because I probably wouldn't have wanted to.' She snapped the words at them with uncharacteristic rudeness.

Then, as she turned away, she caught a glimpse of the reaction in the man's face. He looked as startled as if someone had woken him roughly for a long sleep.

His strange response irritated her even more. Had no one ever spoken rudely to him before today? His accent told her he was a tourist, and she doubted, if he was staying in Broome, it would be the last time it happened. Tempers frayed easily in the sultry summer season here in the north-west of Australia. The hot, heavy, still air was full of foreboding as thunderstorms built up then dumped inches of water on the parched land with a ferocity that seemed like vengeance. Cyclones were born far out over the Indian Ocean, then swerved erratically along the coast, their cat-and-mouse tactics tightening the tension in the locals.

'We wanted to charter a plane to fly over some of the wild country you've got here. Someone said this little Cessna was usually available.' He made the remark into the air between them as if he didn't want to be caught talking to her.

'This plane has already been taken,' she said carefully. 'If you enquire at your hotel, they'll give you details of what's available. Pilots don't sit at the airport waiting for stray tourists to come out and flag down their plane.'

Was it her uneasiness about the hired Cessna that was making her so scratchy? Or were the strangers' remarks still rankling?

'Perhaps if you speak to the owner, Jack, they'll alter

their arrangements,' the woman suggested, deliberately speaking loudly enough for Gaby to hear. 'After all, you'd be willing to pay well.'

The assumption that money could work miracles aggravated her even more.

'You cannot have this plane,' she repeated slowly, so that even the most dense of tourists could understand, then she swung away from them again.

There was a muted discussion before the couple followed her back towards the airport buildings, and, ashamed of her brusqueness, she slowed her steps so that they could catch up with her.

'Most of the charter companies close at this time of the year, so there's not much choice available,' she offered. 'We don't get many tourists in the north-west in the wet season.'

'See, there's nothing doing here.' The woman changed tack suddenly, her voice lightened by the thought of escape from the unwelcoming tropical summer. 'Let's head back to Perth and fly home for some cold weather. Couldn't we, Jack? Wouldn't it be fun?'

She was cajoling him, like a mother tempting a child with the offer of a treat, and Gaby shrugged impatiently at this attitude of pandering to a grown man. She was sorry she had tried to make amends for her rudeness.

'You go, Lauren,' the man responded, with such a deep weariness in his voice that Gaby slid her gaze sideways to have a closer look at him.

His face was hard, straight-profiled, and undeniably handsome, but his skin was unhealthily pale, and pain or suffering of some kind had etched deep lines into his cheeks and furrowed his brow. There were threads of silver in the thick dark hair, and a tiny muscle jumped at the corner of his eye.

As if alerted to her scrutiny by some sixth sense, he turned towards her, and the blue eyes caught and held hers for a moment. Ancestry she never thought of did the rest, and a certainty that this man's life would be bound up in hers filled her with a deep foreboding.

She strode away, close to running. It was the humid weather, the sense of the impending storm! Something was stirring the intuitiveness she rarely felt and never acknowledged. She shivered in the fast-falling dusk, and wiped away the beads of perspiration that had formed on her brow.

The man was a tourist—and about to move on if his wife had anything to do with it! And she was leaving Broome in the morning. He might as well be a visitor from another planet, for all the chance she had of running into him again.

At first her thoughts were panicky, until another notion edged away the fear. She should be glad her inner sense had linked his life with hers, she told herself firmly. It proved how wrong intuition could be, and, if it was wrong about the man, it was probably wrong about the plane as well.

Having reached that satisfactory conclusion, she continued, jauntily, on her way.

'What time do you want to leave in the morning?' Fred asked as she slipped into the north-western hangar.

'As close to sun-up as we can get away. I've a clinic flight scheduled, and I've asked Carole to meet me at Derby airport at seven. Even allowing for her usual grumbling about early morning flights, we could still be on our way by seven-thirty.'

Fred nodded, and Gaby felt his unspoken criticism. If she hadn't had her strange 'fancy' about the plane, they would have flown back to Derby this afternoon and she could have taken off from there at six.

'Cyclone Elvie's only one hundred and fifty miles off the coast and still moving east,' he warned, but Gaby shook her head, dismissing the unspoken warning. It was the plane, not the weather that had been worrying her.

'We've had three lows build up to cyclone intensity so far this summer and every one of them has switched direction before reaching the coast. You know they could follow that pattern all season.'

'I know they can change direction without warning as well, and that a clinic flight could be put off for a week,' Fred argued. 'Those kids out there aren't going to mind if their needles are a week late.'

He grinned and she had to smile back at him. The children on the outlying properties and aboriginal settlements would be overjoyed if the flying nurse never arrived!

'It's Christmas in ten days and we all want time off, Fred. If we cancel this trip, it disrupts the schedule next week, and who knows when the weather is going to worsen enough to stop all but emergency flights?'

Was Fred's doubt about the flight influenced by her insistence that he check the plane so thoroughly, or was the approaching cyclone his only cause for concern?

'You could take one of the Kingairs when we get back to Derby,' he suggested, as if in answer to her thoughts.

'That would be a great idea!' she mocked. 'And if there's an emergency that requires a plane that will take a doctor, nurse and stretcher-case, you can explain to the boss why I'm flying it on a clinic flight! He's already grumbling about having to hire the Cessna while our C90's out of action; he'd be thrilled to think I've left it sitting on the runway and taken off in one of the other Kingairs!'

'No need to get sassy!' Fred grumbled. 'Especially as it was this weird feeling of yours that got me churned up in the first place!'

'The feeling's gone now,' she assured him. 'It probably wasn't intuition but something I ate for lunch.'

She chuckled at the disgust in the old man's face.

'You know there's a heap of stuff they want us to take back?' He ignored her levity, and brought the conversation back to the job they had to do.

Gaby nodded.

'Five cases of medical equipment and one case of the latest emergency rations someone has donated for us to carry on all flights,' she explained. 'It seems there's a new dried-food company anxious to promote its product so they've made up these dinky little parcels of food that don't take up as much room as our old emergency supplies but would keep an army alive for ten years!'

'You wouldn't laugh about it if you were stranded somewhere for a week with no food.'

'But that would never happen in this day and age, would it, Fred? With helicopters on most cattle properties and hundreds of planes in the north-west, how long could you possibly stay lost? It's not like Queensland where the tropical rainforest could hide a plane wreck for months.'

'Well, you never know!' Fred told her crossly. 'And

you shouldn't laugh at the donations people give us. I sometimes think everything's one big joke to you.'

Not quite everything, Gaby thought, but it's certainly easier to laugh than to cry.

'I never laugh at medical donations although I sometimes wonder at the number of metal spare parts surgical companies give us,' she told him soothingly. 'I was waiting for a clearance the other day and tidied the stock cupboard at the base. I reckon we could fit new hips to half the population of the East Kimberleys with the stuff we've got.'

'And one specialist who could do it, and he only comes once every two months and tells the folks with bad hips they'll have to go south for an operation!' Fred agreed.

'But the service we *can* provide is tremendous, and you know it, Fred. Sixty years ago, people on isolated properties had no help at all if they were seriously ill or injured. They got better or they died and that was that. Now we'll stop arguing or I'll be standing here all night! Do you want a lift back to town?'

'Not me. I've had enough of your driving today to last me a lifetime. I'll walk back. I'm staying with Bert Sorenson and his missus tonight.'

Gabby nodded. 'See you in the morning, then,' she said, and punched him lightly but affectionately on the shoulder. He was a good friend and a kind mentor as well as being a genius with planes. All the pilots in the Royal Flying Doctor Service knew that their lives depended on the ability of these dedicated men on the ground, but Fred was more than a mechanic to her, and she valued his concern about her welfare.

As she walked back to her car she saw the Americans leave the main terminal building, also turning towards the car park. Had they been arranging their flight back to Perth?

Walking about twenty yards behind them, she could hear the woman's voice but not the words, although a certain shrill insistence seemed to indicate that an argument was taking place.

The woman, blonde and good-looking in what Gaby thought of as an American way, moved with a smooth assurance but the man walked with a stiff-legged gait, as if he was making a deliberate effort to slow his steps. Tension seemed to radiate from him—his stocky body unable to contain all the energy it produced.

He's a very unhappy man!

The thought was as clear as a voice in her head, and Gaby frowned. Why on earth should she be making that kind of assumption? And she didn't know the man, so why did it matter anyway?

Puzzled by her subconscious interest, she studied his back, summing him up physically in an attempt to banish the mental waywardness of her thoughts.

About five ten or eleven, she guessed, although his solid bulk promoted a first impression of a shorter man. Shoulders like a front-row forward—or whatever the equivalent of that was in American football! Big and wide and hard—that much was obvious from the way his cotton knit shirt stretched across his back. His legs, or what was visible of them below the neat linen shorts, were also well-muscled, although his skin was pale beneath the covering mat of dark hair.

Yet he didn't seem at ease in his casual clothes, and his steps lacked the spring of the athleticism his body implied. Plastic musles, built up in a gym for show, not use? Gaby wondered, before she caught the uncharitableness of the thought and shook her head to chase away her cynicism.

Think about the flight tomorrow, she told herself as the couple crossed the car park and stopped by a car that carried the logo of the Cable Beach Club. Not only tourists, but wealthy tourists!

She turned away to open the door of the rental car she'd driven down from Derby, fragmented images of the man who seemed ill at ease in his own skin still dancing in her mind.

'Phone message for you to call Cable Beach, Gaby. Your dad's in town.' Betty Simpson, manager of the hotel that the RFDS used for staff who were in Broome on business, greeted her with this news as she walked in.

Gaby's first reaction was a wide smile of delight. It was months since she'd seen her father! Her second reaction was spoken aloud. 'And how did he know I was in Broome?'

'How does anyone know anything in this place?' Betty flung out her arms in mock-despair, then bustled away, leaving Gaby to phone from the booth in the lobby.

'I've been down to get Sam from school. He and I are overnighting at Cable Beach, love. You'll join us for dinner?' Her father's voice boomed into her ear. Half a lifetime of shouting into unpredictable pedal wireless then radio-phone links had not been eradicated by the invention of the new DRCS phone systems for the outback. Her father still believed that you had to yell to be heard.

'I didn't see the Piper at the airport,' she said, still

finding it hard to believe that they could both be in Broome on the same day.

'Hangared it in case the weather blew up,' he replied laconically. 'Now, dinner?'

'I'm flying early in the morning, Dad,' she objected, although she knew she would go.

'So am I,' he argued, 'but that's never stopped me having dinner the night before. What time are you leaving and where are you heading? There's another cyclone building up, you know.'

'Back to Derby, then out on a regular clinic flight, three stations, two south and one west of Gibb River. If Elvie continues towards the coast on her present course she'll hit north of there, more Wyndham way.'

'I'll get another weather report before you get here. We'll talk about it then.'

There was a sharp click, then the buzzing sound confirmed that her father had dropped the receiver back into the cradle. Conversation finished!

I hadn't agreed to go to dinner, Gaby thought crossly as she hung up, but they both knew she would go. No matter how he infuriated her, no matter how his transference of allegiance from her to Sam had hurt her, she loved the rough, bluff man who was her father, and would go further than the few miles down the road to Cable Beach to see him whenever she had the opportunity.

And what did he think she was going to wear to the elegant Cable Beach Club for dinner? The shorts she'd worn down in the car from Derby, or her RFDS pilot's uniform?

'Betty?' she called, and heard an answering shout from the region of the hotel's kitchen.

Following the sound, she located her friend.

'Can I borrow something to wear out with Dad tonight?'

Betty's reply was a deep chuckle.

'I'm a stone heaver and four inches taller than you, Gaby, but if you look on my desk in the office you'll find the key to the boutique next door. I'm minding it this week. Duck in there and find something—if you don't spill your soup on it, you can pop it back when you get home.'

Was she joking or not? Gaby wondered as she assured Betty that she would buy whatever she found and hurried off.

Most of the clothes were designed for tall women with thin, sylph-like figures, she decided, before pulling out a plain dress in midnight-blue silk. Its cut was more sophisticated than the clothes she usually wore, but its simple elegance flattered her petite figure and it would please her father to see her out of jeans or shorts.

She showered then dressed carefully, enjoying the feel of the cool silk against her skin. The neckline was cut low, showing the slight cleft between her creamy breasts, and the skirt fitted snugly into her waist then followed the rounded contours of her hips with a flattering femininity. Exactly how her father liked to picture his only daughter, she decided as she looked critically at her reflection.

Then she sighed. Pleasing her father was one thing, but she knew her appearance was unlikely to divert him totally. She would still be on the receiving end of a lecture. Grimacing at the thought, she rubbed cream between her fingertips then smoothed it into her skin, seeing the sparkle of excitement in her eyes and the flush of pleasure colouring her cheeks.

The face of the north-west, her father used to say,

taking her by the chin and turning her face towards his guests.

She supposed he was right, although her own features were too familiar for her to analyse. Chinese, Malay and aboriginal blood all ran through her veins, diluted by intermarriage with Europeans in every generation until it took a certain angle or a particular shift of the light for actual racial characteristics to become apparent in anything but the bottomless pools of darkness that were her eyes, and the slanting cheekbones that gave her face an exotic cast.

Cable Beach Club was a luxury resort nestling in acres of tropical gardens by the long, sandy beach of the same name. As Gaby made her way along the discreetly lit paths to the bungalow her father used when he was in town she breathed in the richly scented night air, and wondered if a life of pampered luxury would be all bad.

'Gaby!'

Sam erupted like a cannonball from the front door, hugging her with all the enthusiasm and joy of his childhood. Then he remembered that he was now a teenager, and 'cool', and he dropped back a step and asked, 'How's things, Sis?' in the bored tone he had developed to suit his image.

'Pretty good, Scrappy,' she replied with a smile, equally casual although her eyes feasted on him, noticing how tall he was growing—and how like her father!

She'd been eight years old when he was born prematurely on the property. The RFDS had flown in a thermacot humidicrib and saved the little scrap of humanity, pumping plasma into her mother to keep her alive on the flight back to Wyndham, where surgery had been necessary to remove the placenta and tidy up the damage that the birth had done.

It had been three months before the pair had returned home, and, when they did, Scrappy had become Gaby's special project. Any free time she had was spent with the baby, talking to him, showing him things, singing songs, or carting him around the house and yards, unknowingly providing the extra stimulation that his underdeveloped brain and body needed to catch up to a normal growth curve.

'Sam's not joining us for dinner. He's got a mate with him and they've opted for steak and chips in the room while they watch a video.'

Her father's eyes shone as they rested on her. They might argue about her lifestyle, and fight about her place in his plans for the future, but there was a special bond between them that would never be broken.

Gaby walked with him through the mellow night, feeling the humidity like a soft shawl around her shoulders, smiling while he talked of Teralga, and the cattle, the sales, the men, the new Ultra-light he'd bought for mustering, and the plans he'd made for sitting out the wet.

It was familiar talk, and the security it provided overwhelmed her as they came to the lighted restaurant and he guided her inside.

'It *is* good to see you, Dad,' she said, standing on tiptoe to kiss him on the cheek, the love she felt for this man lighting her whole body.

He slid an arm around her shoulders, and drew her close against his chest for a moment, his hug telling her all she needed to know.

'Well, pardon us!' a crisp voice said behind them,

and Gaby spun out of the embrace to face the woman who had annoyed her at the airport earlier.

An insolent green glance flickered from her father's face to hers, then skimmed down over the lush body that had been hidden by her uniform earlier in the day. The woman's thoughts were easier to read than the lines in a comic book, and Gaby felt rare anger burning through her again. Her father, oblivious as ever to external impressions, was apologising for blocking the entrance and waving the American couple past with a courtly bow.

It was the man who caught Gaby's venomous glare, and again she saw a startled look in the piercing blue eyes that met hers for an instant as he passed.

'They think I'm your mistress,' she hissed at her father when he took her hand to lead her to the table he had booked.

'Think an old fellow like me could win a beauty like you, Gaby?' he asked, amused by her contention.

'Fifty's not old!' she protested. 'You're a handsome devil and you know it, James Forsythe! Add the fact that you've got pots of money to the good looks and you couldn't lose.'

'Well, it's lucky I still love your mother to distraction, or I might get into all kinds of trouble.' He watched the American couple settle at a table near by. 'Although ice-cold Nordic beauties like that one never did appeal to me. Shall we play up to them?'

He grinned wickedly at her, and looked so like Sam when he was plotting mischief that she chuckled in reply.

'Why not?' she purred, leaning across the table towards him and running her slim fingers along his hand. 'You can tell me how Mum is and what she's planning for Christmas, and let them think you're bribing me into your bed with another yacht and a new mink coat.'

She spoke lightly, but the presence of the man with the blue eyes was like a physical force, clanging against her senses with a jolting insistence.

'Did I ever tell you how I met your mother?' her father asked, and she bit back the, Only one thousand times, she was about to reply. She loved the story, but wouldn't have to listen with total attention, and, while he told it, she could try to work out why the stranger was affecting her like this.

'Just knew, she said, and couldn't explain it more. It was something inside her, she insisted, told her the moment we met that I would be bound up in her life.'

Her father's use of the same word that had struck her earlier brought her out of her preoccupation and back to the present. Had he always used the word 'bound' when he'd recounted the story? She couldn't remember!

As he continued she turned her head away, forgetting her earlier determination to play the part of the devoted mistress, and again met the intent scrutiny of the man who was disrupting her inner calm and clouding her thoughts.

He's not *that* good-looking, she decided as she swung back to bestow a glittering smile on her father. Too harsh—too disillusioned, somehow! Too pale! And, to make things worse, one eyebrow was cocked permanently upwards—giving an impression of a cynicism that made her shudder.

'You've probably got too much of my blood in you to share your mother's intuition,' her father was saying.

'I most certainly have,' she told him stoutly. 'Mum's

"feelings" have always given me the heebie-jeebies. I want none of that nonsense in my life.'

Watching her father's face, she saw the warmth fade slightly, as if his skin had tightened in reaction to her flippant words.

'She's often right, Gaby, love,' he reminded her. 'She. . .' He shook his head, as if to thrust away the thought he'd been about to share, then smiled at her again. 'But now let's talk about you. Are you ready to throw in this piloting nonsense and come home to give your old parents a hand on the farm?'

'You mean come home and play ladies with the flying north-west social set,' she teased. 'What else is there for me to do? You have more help than you know what to do with on the "farm" and Mum is happily involved with her silversmithing, now Sam's gone off to boarding-school.'

Her father nodded his agreement, then reached out and took her hand—but not for show this time!

'I miss you out there, Gaby,' he said, in a low, gruff tone that tore into her heart. 'Miss you with me when I ride out, miss you when I fly, miss having you to talk to when things bother me.'

'Teralga will be Sam's, Dad; we've all agreed on that. You'd lose the heart of the place if you tried to divide it between us.' She spoke huskily through the pain she still felt at what she saw as rejection. 'I've got to stop loving it the way I did when I thought it would be mine, and I can't do that if I'm there all the time.'

'Well, go to Perth,' he suggested. 'Live in the house there and lead a life more suited to a young woman with your wealth and beauty. Do things, meet people, find a young man to marry and give me grandchildren.'

'I do things in Derby,' she said, sighing at the

predictability of this argument they always had. 'And I meet plenty of people.'

Including ones I'd rather not have met, she added silently, as she sensed a movement at the other table and the irritability she was feeling strained against her nerves once again.

'Doctors or sick people,' her father muttered in disgust, then sat back as the waiter slid a plate of grilled tuna on to the table in front of him.

The arrival of the food diverted him, and they finished their meal with small talk about the coming Christmas festivities, before getting on to the new breeding programme he was trying with the cattle.

It had to be chance that decreed that they leave the restaurant at the same time as the Americans.

'Good evening,' the man said, his voice polite as he studied her with an openness that made her want to hit him. Didn't he know it was rude to stare?

'Good evening,' she muttered, hoping her father wouldn't give way to his innate bush friendliness and start talking to them.

She took his arm, aiming to deter any polite overtures, and tried to steer him out of the door, but the blonde woman was speaking, and her father paused politely. Behind her right shoulder, she could feel the man watching her.

'I believe I know you,' the woman was saying to her father, with the incredulous tone of someone discovering a bizarre coincidence. 'Didn't I meet you at the Saxons' place in Texas last year?'

Gaby sighed her relief. Her father had many friends in the United States, and visited each year to discuss cattle breeding and investigate new blood lines, but the Saxons were not on his list of top ten favourite people.

On a recent visit to Teralga, they had displayed a rare
and subtle racism towards her mother for which he
would never forgive them.

'I don't believe I know them,' he replied shortly, and
now it was he who steered Gaby out of the door.
'Dreadful people,' he muttered as they walked through
the balmy night towards the car park.

Was he talking about the Saxons or the two
Americans, now judged and labelled by such a tenuous
association?

CHAPTER TWO

'THERE was a message for you from Derby to say you'll have a passenger in the morning. Mike said he'd told the fellow to be at the airport by sun-up.'

Gaby nodded as Betty imparted this information. Two more hands to load and unload the supplies she had to carry. It was a reflex action for her mind to calculate the extra weight a passenger would mean. Assuming his weight was seventy-five kilos, to be on the safe side, she would be shaving the weight limit if she filled her tanks before take-off.

That's OK, she told herself, dipping her head as the decision was made. I'll have to fill up at Derby anyway, so I'll carry less out of Broome. She stripped off, showered, and fell into bed, excited—as she always was—about the prospect of real work in the morning.

Headlights cut the pre-dawn darkness from a car in front of her on the road to the airport. Fred would be walking, her father wouldn't leave this early, so presumably it was her passenger—unless there was another pilot in town who liked to be in the air to meet the sun as it rose in its brazen splendour over the flat plains to the east.

The other car turned into one of the spaces reserved for hire cars, and she parked beside it. As she pushed open the door and stood up, she knew it was the American who was locking the car beside hers. Not intuition this time, but the smell of male cologne wafting through the warm air. A sharp scent, yet subtle in its undertones. Nothing like the aftershave any of the men she knew would favour!

'I believe I drop the keys to this rental car through a hole in the front door of the air terminal building.' The husky voice came out of the darkness and slid into Gaby's soul.

Don't be stupid, she warned herself, before answering him.

'I'm dropping my keys through. It's this way.'

She walked away, not waiting for him although she was certain he was going to be her passenger.

'I'm looking for the Royal Flying Doctor Service pilot,' he said as he caught up with her.

'That's me,' she muttered, as his voice and presence acted on her nerves like a wire brush, rasping them to an uncomfortable rawness she could not handle.

When they reached the well-lit building, Gaby turned and offered her hand, going through the motions of acting normally in the hope that whatever was happening inside her would be fooled and settle back down.

'Gaby Forsythe!' she introduced herself, and heard him draw in a sharp breath. Then his hand, cool and dry, closed around hers.

'The exotic beauty from the Beach Club,' he murmured, with too much flippant admiration in his tone for it to be a compliment.

'The pilot your wife mistook for a stewardess,' she reminded him coldly, and drew her hand back, as if, by that simple physical movement, she could reclaim the ground she could feel herself losing to this man.

He shook his head, and again she had the strange

impression that behind the hard mask of his face he was carrying a great burden of some kind.

'I'm Jack Fletcher,' he said.

'What do you weigh?'

She blurted out the question because attempting to assess his weight meant that she had to look at him, and she couldn't bring herself to study the hard-packed muscle and sturdy frame too closely.

'One-seventy.'

The figure meant nothing to her, but Fred, joining them at that moment, translated.

'Bit over twelve stone or seventy-five kilos. You'll be well under weight, Gaby,' he told her. 'I left the tanks half-empty because you'll have to fill up at Derby anyway.'

She turned away from the man to greet Fred and introduce him.

'This way—we've some gear to load,' Fred said briskly. He led the way to the north-western hangar and unlocked the door.

'The bigger planes from down south don't fly into Derby—strip's shorter than this,' Fred explained, loading the passenger's arms with boxes. 'This stuff usually goes by road but as we were going up anyway we decided to take it.'

Gaby picked up a large carton and led the way out of the hangar and across the tarmac to where the little Cessna stood.

'Put them down here,' she told the men, setting her own burden down on the ground beside the plane. 'I'll stack it in.'

'Some of these boxes are heavy,' Jack Fletcher objected, and Gaby slanted an old-fashioned look at him.

'On the ground!' she repeated. 'No one packs a plane I fly but me.'

She would have liked to ask which one he considered heavy, then lift it easily to confuse him, although she didn't understand why the man was bringing out all the aggressive traits in her nature.

He walked away, back for another load, and she carefully stowed the boxes, testing each one and placing it carefully so that the plane would be balanced in flight.

'If you sit behind me, Fred, and you—Jack—up front.' She hesitated before using his name, as if naming him would make him more of a person. Yet she could hardly ignore him for the hour's flight back to Derby.

The two men clambered in while she walked around the plane once more, removing the control locks and doing a last visual check.

The interior of the plane had diminished to matchbox proportions, she realised as she settled into her seat, with the stranger's bulk in the seat beside her. She watched him fasten his seatbelt, then handed him a headset.

'The intercom within the plane is voice-activated,' she explained. 'You can speak to Fred or me through that, and you'll hear our conversation. OK?'

The man looked at her, nodding his understanding, while searching her face in the pale rosy light of the summer dawn. Held by his scrutiny, she studied him in turn, noticing the little scar above his right eyebrow that gave it the lifted look. He's still a cynical devil, she told herself, even if the raised eyebrow isn't caused by a perpetual sneer.

'Just visiting Derby?' Fred asked as she started the engine and headed down the runway.

'I'd heard about your Flying Doctors back home, and, being in Broome, it seemed silly to be this close and not see something of the operation.'

'You a doctor?' Fred's questioning continued as Gaby lifted the little plane easily into the air.

'I'm supposed to be,' the man replied obscurely. Glancing quickly towards him, Gaby saw the thin lips set into a straight line.

Then, as they rose higher, the roaring red fire that was the sun came into view, turning the bare earth beneath to purple, orange and vermilion brilliance. She turned the plane away from the blinding glare, but the man looked back, sucking air in through his teeth as if the sight of such flagrant beauty had stolen his ability to breathe.

'Pretty, ain't it?' Fred remarked, and Gaby saw the man's head shake sideways, a silent admission that no word could describe such a display. His face had softened, and he looked handsome again. Was the beauty of nature's show easing some of the tension she felt emanating from him?

'Is that why you take off so early?' he asked, when the colour had faded and the blue sea and white beachline to the west had caught his attention.

'I've still a full days's clinic flight ahead of me. If I left any later, I'd be running behind time all day,' she replied prosaically, not wanting to share with this man how special that burst of beauty was to her innermost being.

'Practical as well as beautiful,' he remarked, and she thought he sounded disappointed.

Rubbish, she chided herself. The man's not thinking of you as a person at all!

'I'm a pilot doing a job,' she said with a dismissive shrug. She hoped he would realise that she didn't want his facile and insincere compliments, and would talk to Fred if he wanted to talk.

She turned her attention back to the plane, completing her top-of-climb checks, then radioed her take-off time, immediate destination and ETA. With the formalities over, she listened to the engine throbbing steadily, relishing the way the plane handled and the lightness of the controls.

'You happy with the way she's handling now she's airborne?' Fred asked, as if sensing her thoughts.

'She's a lovely plane,' Gaby assured him. 'And with the modified set-back doors that let passengers get in without clambering over the front seats she's ideal for some of our RFDS work.'

Yet even as she spoke her mind did a mental scan to see if the strange premonitory feeling she'd had yesterday was still lurking somewhere.

She felt nothing that could disturb her peace—except the presence of their extra passenger. Maybe he was what the strange feeling had been about! Less frightening than a plane malfunction, she told herself, then turned to look at him. His eyes met hers, as if by some pre-arranged signal, and she wondered.

'Think the bosses back in Victoria might think about buying a little one like this for odd jobs?' Fred asked.

'Not until they've replaced——'

'Victoria?'

They spoke together, and, as Gaby turned towards Jack Fletcher, he waved a hand for her to continue.

'The Flying Doctor Service was imagined then set up

by a man named Flynn who was born in Victoria,' she explained, answering the question she'd heard in the single word. 'Because Victoria is such a small state, they don't need a service like this, so the people there, fired by one man's dreams, adopted the most remote bit of Australia, the Kimberleys, here in Western Australia, as their section, way back in 1934. The people and businesses of Victoria provide the resources and manage Derby base.'

'And at the moment they're replacing aircraft?' he asked, finishing her own statement.

'Exactly! Queensland section trialled the Beechcraft Super Kingair C200s and C90s as replacements for the old Queenairs. They found them more cost-effective, so now everyone's clamouring for new planes.'

'And you don't approve?'

She looked sharply at him, unable to believe he could have picked up her doubt from the crisp statement.

'I happen to think there's a use in every fleet for smaller planes as well,' she said. 'The planes got bigger as more and more equipment was added. Some are like a flying intensive-care unit, but emergencies shouldn't be the primary focus on the service. A small, single-engined craft like this would be useful for the simple health services that are part of preventative medicine.'

'Wouldn't engine capability come into it? Two engines must surely be better than one.'

He argued like a man used to being right!

'I don't agree,' she said tartly. 'It might have been the case when engines were more unreliable, but with all the modern refinements in aircraft manufacture today, and the increased number of all-weather strips in the bush, not to mention the improved roads to land on in emergencies, the only real risk is pilot error.'

'But what about take-off and landing if you've an engine malfunction? Impossible with a single engine.' The question was a deliberate goad!

'Try it with one engine in a twin-engined plane some time,' she suggested, 'on an isolated dirt strip, with a cross-wind reading that's guesswork and four people on board. The secret is having planes that are so well-serviced and checked that mechanical failure doesn't occur.'

And I should flip this little baby over to give him a fright, she thought, annoyed that he was arguing with her as well as irritating her with his presence.

She checked her watch instead, trying to divert her mind from its preoccupation with the stranger. They were making good time in spite of the strengthening winds that were beginning to play rough games of push and pull with the plane. Far away to the north-west she could see the band of cloud that denoted the edge of Elvie, but its menace seemed unreal as she flew through the cloud-free blue and golden morning. And the closer menace would be dispensed with in another half an hour, she realised.

Fred was explaining about the equipment their own planes carried. Had the man asked a question and she had missed it? Not that it mattered—she didn't want to talk to him anyway.

'And what's a clinic flight?' he asked when Fred had finished, and Gaby knew that Fred would expect her to reply.

'It's a regular flight, usually with just a nurse on board, to carry out immunisation against diphtheria, whooping cough, tetanus and polio. She does prenatal checks for pregnant women, weighs babies, tends to minor wounds or infections, checks on convalescing patients, and sees people who may have already been treated by the doctor over the phone——'

'Whoa up a bit, lady! This takes some absorbing.'

Gaby turned at the interruption, and surprised a look of interest on his face.

He looks quite nice when he's not frowning! The thought slipped through her defences before she had time to clang them closed again.

'Which bit?' she asked.

'Well!' The word was drawled, and the slowness emphasised the American accent and the huskiness of his voice. 'I'm with you on the kids' shots, but the rest of the stuff. You don't take a doctor? And how does he treat people over the phone?'

Gaby chuckled. To outsiders, the scope of RFDS was sometimes overwhelming, although the actual operation was simplified through years of refinement.

'Every family living more than eighty kilometres from a doctor is entitled to have a government medical chest,' she explained, 'although many families that close opt not to keep one——'

'That close?' he queried, but she had already launched into the next part of the story.

'All the items in the chest are numbered, and there is also a chart of the front and back of the human body with numbers corresponding to different parts.'

'So I phone your base and say I've got a sharp pain in number three, and he prescribes two of number one hundred and sixty-four three times a day!'

'Something like that,' Gaby agreed, glancing sideways at this man who was too sharp for his own good. Few people accepted the simplicity of the strange medical arrangement so quickly. 'Except that three is your left shoulder and heart region and you wouldn't need anaesthetic eyedrops for that!' That should put him back in his place, she thought.

'How many items in this chest?' The questioning continued as he ignored her dig.

'About two hundred,' she told him, wondering why he was so interested.

'And do you know each and every one by number?' he enquired. 'Are you a trained nurse as well as a pilot?'

His voice teased at her nerve-endings, still flayed by his presence.

'I grew up with a chest in the house,' she told him, but didn't add that she'd learnt to count numbering off the little bottles and packages in the chest that had been like a magical toy to a child who had no playmates.

'That's Derby ahead,' she said, pointing to the small township that nestled on the edge of the broad sound. Then she concentrated on the plane, shutting Jack Feltcher out of her thoughts with the practicalities of landing safely.

'It will certainly be an interesting day,' he murmured, at the exact moment that she drew back on the stick to level the plane for touchdown.

The words jolted through her and Fred muttered crossly as the plane skipped and hopped along the tarmac, her inattention making her bungle the landing as badly as a novice pilot on her first attempt.

'If you unload, I'll bring the fuel-tender over and take the boxes back on it.'

Fred was issuing instructions while she taxied towards their hangar.

'Carole will have gear to load as well,' she reminded him. 'Her own equipment and the usual emergency stuff, plus whatever last-minute supplies people have phoned in to ask us to bring out for them. I hope someone's weighed it.'

She unsnapped her seatbelt, ignoring the passenger. Surely his words didn't mean he was to accompany them on the clinic flight? Visiting doctors were sometimes invited to join a non-essential flight but this man wasn't even certain he was a doctor. And she didn't want him sitting next to her all day!

Mike Evans walked towards them, a welcoming smile on his face that certainly wasn't for her and Fred. Mike was a busy, dedicated doctor with a commitment to the bush and the Service, but his clashes with his female pilot in recent times had dimmed a little of the joy and excitement that Gaby had always felt in her job.

'Jack Fletcher?' Mike called as the visitor extricated himself from the plane.

'And there goes the extra hand with the unlaoding,' Gaby said bitterly as the two men walked away.

Mike believed that the planes should work as hard as he did, that gear loaded and unloaded itself, and that if he could function with little or no sleep, so could a pilot. Sometimes Gaby suspected that he also believed the word pilot was a masculine noun and flying planes an exclusively male ability.

'He's having a bad time at the moment, Gaby,' Fred excused their boss as he helped her lift the heavier boxes to the ground before heading off to bring the fuel-tender across to the plane. 'He was annoyed with us yesterday when I rang to say I was doing a full service and we'd be overnighting in Broome. "Fiddling around wasing time," he called it.'

'But he knows the planes have to be mechanically sound, and that Civil Aviation regulations govern the hours we fly. What would happen to the Service if all the pilots lost their licences?'

'He remembers the days when we had a steady stream of well-trained pilots on loan from the big airlines and there was always a pilot available when he needed one. Added to that, he's been as bitter as hell since Mary went back down south with the kids and left him on his own up here. He's not a happy man, and you know it.'

Gaby nodded once, admitting that Fred's explanation was both fair and true.

'But it doesn't make it any easier to work for him these days, Fred,' she said. This one annoyance spoilt an otherwise perfect occupation.

In spite of the lack of help, they were ready to take off again in half an hour. Carole had packed all her equipment on to the small trailer attached to the tender, so it came out with the fuel, and Gaby stayed by the plane and re-packed it, knowing she was anxious to avoid a confrontation with Mike.

'Right, let's go,' she said to Carole as soon as the last parcel was stowed.

'But you haven't given Mike your flight plan or got the latest weather bulletin,' Carole objected. 'And I believe we've got a passenger. Some doctor from the States.'

Gaby's heart sank. The man *was* coming with them.

'You could drop this over for me and pick up the bulletin and the passenger,' she suggested to Carole, who pulled a face in reply and tipped her head commandingly towards the office.

'I'll be five minutes,' Gaby said, giving in to the unspoken order, 'so you get yourself settled and ready for take-off. If the passenger isn't prepared to get a move on, we'll go without him.'

She raced across the tarmac, and slipped into the radio-room, hoping she could carry out her pre-flight procedure without seeing Mike—or the man who was supposed to be her passenger for the day.

They were both there—obviously waiting for her. Mike smiled genially and explained about their visitor—being nice because he knew she didn't want to take the man! Gaby surmised.

'You might include Kulumburu if you've time,' he suggested. 'Show Jack a mission station while he's here.'

'I'll see how we're going,' she responded non-committally. If Carole was held up at any of her clinic stops, the extra distance to the mission would be impossible, but she wasn't going to argue with Mike in front of Jack Fletcher.

She crossed to the desk and picked up her schedule and the weather forecast, noting that Elvie was still continuing on an easterly track and was now only a hundred miles off the coast. The winds would strengthen as they flew north but with the small plane she would be able to land into them on all three strips.

'Let's go!'

It wasn't the warmest of invitations, she realised, when she saw the shocked expression on Mike's face. If he thought the American doctor was some kind of god, to be treated with deference and awe, then he should have asked one of the other pilots to take him for a free ride.

She strode away, but the man's longer legs soon brought him alongside her. He measured his pace to hers.

'Do you always object to taking a passenger or am I an exception?'

The question halted her mid-stride, then she hurried on, hoping he hadn't noticed.

'I didn't say I didn't want to take you,' she replied.

'You didn't have to, lady. Since the moment we met you've been sending out "stand clear of me" signals that are so strong, they make words superfluous.'

'Don't be ridiculous,' she argued, but the words lacked the conviction they needed.

He shrugged, and moved imperceptibly closer, and immediately she dropped her clipboard. Stooping to retrieve it, she knew her body had reacted to his movement. Had he been trying to prove his point?

'When we take off I'll switch your earphones so you can talk to Carole during the flight. The radio will be chattering and I try to concentrate on that so I know who else is in the air around us.'

'Don't talk to me and I won't talk to you, eh?'

It was her turn to shrug. She waved him towards the passenger side of the plane, and watched him climb in, then did a final check and pulled herself up into her seat.

The little plane lifted easily and as she radioed her take-off time and initial destination to the central control tower she felt the familiar lightness of spirit that had filled her since she first handled a joystick at the age of twelve. There was nothing in the world to compare with it, she decided, smiling happily as she set the direction-finder and settled back into her seat. Up here the winds were stronger, so she kept her hands on the controls, gently cradling the craft to minimise the effect of the buffeting.

The murmur of the man's voice made her turn, and she realised that, while he might be talking to Carole, he was watching her. His blue eyes had a strange expression in them, as if she puzzled him.

Not as much as you puzzle me, she could have said, knowing that the strange bond she had felt when they'd first met was still tangling her thoughts and sending messages through her blood.

She looked beyond him to the thick dark edge of cloud with its tattered edges swirling away from it like broad white streamers. Ceiling at two thousand feet if it continued to close in, she remembered. It looked much closer than the hundred miles away of the forecast, but the cloud mass could be spread anything up to a hundred-mile radius from the eye.

Ahead she could see the Charlotte Downs landing strip, with at least eight bush vehicles drawn up alongside it. Red clumps of dust, like coloured cotton balls, rolled towards it—more people coming in to see Carole, or simply to meet each other for a chat.

Checking the wind, she landed easily, taxi-ing towards the small verandaed hut where Carole would run the clinic. Many of the outback properties were providing these facilities now, saving what was often a long drive from the air strip to the homestead, and so cutting back on the time it took for a visit.

Carole unlatched the door on her side and climbed out, pulling her bag after her. Leaving the passenger to make his own arrangements, Gaby followed.

'I'll help you unload.'

She turned in surprise when he spoke, then opened the hatch and reached in behind the seats to get the cool-box that contained the vaccinations and medications.

'If you take this across to the hut, Carole can get started.'

And you can stay and watch her, she told his back as he walked away.

She delved into the luggage compartment again, pulling out the boxes and cartons and stacking them on the ground beside the plane.

'Let me do that!'

The dratted man was back!

He eased her aside with one hand on her arm, and reached his longer arms into the cramped space.

'Wouldn't it be easier to pack the things that get off first on top?' he asked as she sorted through the boxes and began passing some to Bill James, the Charlotte Downs foreman.

'Much easier,' she told him smartly, 'and if I had no concern for my passengers' comfort I'd do that. In case you didn't know, a badly balanced aircraft yaws.'

'I thought that was something people got in the tropics if they weren't too fussy about hygiene,' he quipped, and she looked sharply at him, surprised by the laughter in his voice. A tentative smile chased across his face, and her mind went blank.

The slight spreading of his lips had a lightening effect, which banished the look of strain and tiredness. As the impact of the change began to lessen and thought returned, she realised that she was staring at him—at the different man who stood beside her on the hot, dusty airstrip, brushing at flies and smiling quite openly now.

He's passing through, she told herself, a foreigner and married, but the admonitions had little effect on her body as it pursued a life of its own, sending and receiving messages too inexplicable—too extraordinary—to be put into words.

'There's a cuppa ready for you on the veranda, Gaby,' Bill said as he climbed into his dusty four-wheel drive.

She licked her lips.

'Do you want a cuppa?' she asked her passenger, then realised he might not understand. 'Cup of tea,' she translated, and whisked away from him. 'Over here!'

She swallowed nervously and swatted at the flies while her body hummed with excitement, singing some secret song as if it had suddenly discovered new dimensions of feeling and was gloating over the find.

Not even her first boyfriend, back when she was at school in Perth, had affected her this way, although she remembered a heart-flip or two he had caused.

They were about ten yards from the hut when Carole emerged, one hand shading her eyes from the sun. She spotted them, then hurried across the veranda and into the glare.

'Would you be willing to look at one of these kids?' she asked Jack, and Gaby saw the gleam die out of his eyes and his face become still and hard again.

'He's a passenger, not a doctor, on this flight, Carole,' she objected, feeling transferred pain shifting uneasily in her stomach.

'Doctors are always doctors,' Carole argued, watching the man who had said nothing.

'I've done little general practice medicine for years. I'm a specialist who has spent the last ten years looking at bits of gut rather than at whole people. My looking could raise false hopes.'

'It's only a hernia, and that's guts!' Carole said, her exasperation unhidden. 'I don't know whether we should take the kid back to town for an operation or if he'd be safe to leave until the next doctor's visit after Christmas.'

'And what would you have done if I hadn't been on the flight?' Jack asked her as they all walked up the steps to the veranda.

'I'd have tried gentle external manual manipulation to make sure nothing feels knotted and, because he's a tough little larrikin, probably have dressed it to protect it from outside impact,' Carole told him, then smiled. 'I suppose having even an unofficial medico on board has dented my confidence.'

Now Carole got the rare smile, and Gaby realised that there'd been nothing special in the one she'd witnessed. It was natural that the man could smile, she supposed. After all, most people could!

'I'll have a look. As it is my special area of expertise an epigastric hernia is always of interest, but manipulation won't help much. There's little risk of the intestine becoming trapped or gangrenous if it's umbilical and most will heal spontaneously as the child grows.'

'He's five—is there still a chance of that happening?' Carole asked.

'I would think so,' Jack replied. 'In the States we rarely operate until after a child turns six, unless it's causing pain or other problems.'

They walked off together, disappearing into the hut. Gaby greeted the motley crew of people gathered in the shade, moving from one another with a handshake or quick kiss. She helped herself to a cup of tea and a biscuit from a newly opened packet, then dropped down on to the veranda floor, her legs stretched out in front of her, chatting to Bill's wife about the weather and Christmas and whether the heat and the flies were worse than usual this summer. She was accepted as one of them, born and bred in the north-west, and part of the extended family that inhabited the inhospitable region.

Then Jack Fletcher dropped down to sit beside her and the conversation ceased. It was not politeness, she knew, but an uncertainty about what to say to this stranger from another world.

She looked at his legs, clad in faded jeans like some of the other men, black and white, who stood around. Then her gaze slid upwards. Muscles beneath the denim—the other men had muscles, although on the whole they were leaner and stringier. Blue shirt—there were at least four other faded cotton shirts! Yet he was different—as different as an alpine evergreen among the straggly gums and swollen boabs.

'It's another world,' he murmured quietly, almost voicing her thoughts.

She heaved herself to her feet and carried her cup back to the folding table where the tea things had been set up. If she was further away from him, the inner disturbances might subside.

'Feed the nurse then we'll be off,' Gaby suggested to Ellen James as the little boy with the hernia marched proudly out of the hut, displaying the snowy white bandage on his round brown tummy with inordinate pride.

'Always in a hurry, you lot,' Ellen grumbled, 'and

with phones now instead of radio we women never get a chance for a good gossip.'

'You won't go back home the minute we leave,' Gaby teased, 'so don't try and pretend you will. I reckon this galah session won't be over for a few hours yet.'

'Galah session?' Jack repeated the phrase in a puzzled tone, and suddenly the uneasiness was broken as the men rushed into speech, making fun of the way the women used to speak to each other on the old radios.

'Chattering like a bunch of galahs,' Bill explained. 'Made the air blue with some of the things they passed over those airwaves!'

'A galah is a bird,' Carole told him kindly while she sipped her cup of tea. 'They travel in flocks and make raucous, screeching noises——'

'Quite unlike the woman of the west who are gentle, ladylike and refined!' Gaby added, only to be shouted down with bellowing laughter.

'I've heard you cursing better than your old man, and that's saying something!' one old man claimed.

'And heard you gossiping until your tongue was likely to fall off,' another added.

'I should go and fly planes in Tasmania,' Gaby grumbled, brushing the dirt off the back of her divided skirt. 'I might be appreciated there.'

'They wouldn't have a little thing like you down there. First big snowfall and you'd disappear.'

'I'm leaving now!' she said with a great show of dignity. 'I won't stay here and be insulted by a rabble like you lot. Come along, Nurse!'

She sauntered down the steps then turned around and grinned at the gathering.

'Merry Christmas to you all, in case I'm not back up this way next week,' she said warmly, but the special, loving, all-embracing smile she gave them caught the stranger in their midst, and wavered for an instant as their eyes met again, this time locking together like the cogs of a wheel meshing into place.

CHAPTER THREE

THE edge of cloud had moved closer, and, as Gaby turned the Cessna west towards their next stop, they flew out of the sunshine although the ceiling was still too high to bother them.

'Do you do much clinic work?' Jack asked, and Gaby waited for Carole to reply. When the silence persisted, she turned in her seat, to see the nurse wedged into an uncomfortable position against the window and fast asleep.

'It's always been a big part of the service,' she replied.

'So it's not all guts and glory—flying in the emergency kits and staff, whip in a drip, add a bit of emergency care by the roadside, then a life-depending dash back to a hospital.'

She looked at him, so close in the small cockpit that she could have counted the hairs in his eyebrows.

'Generally speaking, the health of people in the bush is poorer than the health of their city cousins. A large percentage of our flights are emergencies, and next time you're gored by a bull and losing blood by the gallon you might be glad we exist, but preventative medicine is just as important, and that includes teaching people how to look after themselves and their kids. In many cases, it's teaching basic hygiene skills.'

'So how many of these clinic flights might you do in a year?'

Gaby sighed. Carole should be answering all these

questions. She was the longest-serving medical employee at Derby, where the doctors worked on a contract basis from the Health Department.

'Last year we did over five hundred clinic flights, of which approximately half would have been with a doctor. A total of close to ten thousand people attended those clinics, and from them about five hundred would have been transported back to town for further treatment.'

She rattled off the figures but her mind was on her own job, nursing the plane into the wind. She stretched one hand to the radio, seeking the frequency for the latest weather bulletin. If Elvie was still heading for the coast, then a cyclone alert would have started with half-hourly reports coming through.

'You get many rough days like this?'

She glanced at the man to see if the bouncing was affecting him, and was relieved to see that his skin colour looked normal—still pale compared to the men of the tropics, but not sallow or sickly.

'That cloud's the edge of a cyclone,' she told him, waving a hand towards the towering mass that was growing more ominous as their paths converged. 'We get a few each wet season. And when the sky's clear there are thermals out over the desert that can lift or drop a plane fifty feet in a split-second.'

'Sounds like a fun job!'

She looked at him, but there was no smile to make the words a joke.

'I don't do it for fun' she said, 'although I do happen to love it. I'm a professional who has studied hard and learnt the necessary skills—just as you and Carole have in your particular fields.'

She took a bearing, looked around to check that she

was the only idiot flying around on the edge of a big blow, then circled above the dusty plain behind the Windaroo homestead.

Landing the Cessna in the strengthening winds took all her concentration. As they rattled to a stop beside Ted Egan's pick-up truck, Jack Fletcher touched her on the shoulder.

She turned to look at him, but whatever he had been going to say was lost when their glances clashed and held again. Her eyes met with twin pools of blue, the same colour as the sky through which she loved to fly. The world spun slowly round, and she was sucked down into a whirlpool of feeling that had no meaning she could recognize.

'I've a lot of stuff to unload here,' she croaked, reaching back and flipping open the door to reclaim her mind from its senseless meanderings.

'G'day, Gaby,' Ted greeted her as she dropped out of the plane. 'What if I take Carole and her magic box of tricks up to the house, and come back for you and the boyfriend?'

'He's a visiting doctor from the States,' she muttered, blushing a fiery red at the intimation, but Ted was already helping Carole out. He took her bag and the cool-box, loaded them all into the little truck, and Gaby was left with the 'boyfriend'.

'I'm not myself at the moment,' Jack said, startling her almost as much as Ted had.

She lifted out a box and handed it to him, but, rather than lowering it to the ground, he held it, looking at her over the top. 'I could be having a nervous break-down, or suffering a weird reaction from overwork and stress.'

'That's nice for you,' she muttered, taking the box

from him and plonking it down on the ground. 'But why pick Broome to have your crisis?'

She lifted out another parcel and dropped it on the first, infuriated that the man seemed to be excusing something that hadn't happened.

He made no reply.

So they'd looked at each other—so what? she thought, irritated by the deepening silence. It was no big deal, nothing to go blaming on a nervous breakdown, surely!

She pulled packages out with more haste than care, forgetting to separate the ones for Windaroo from those to go back into the plane. Maybe her father was right. Maybe she should go down and live in Perth for a while, meet a few people. She could go out with some of the boys she knew from school—boys who now thought they were men.

Her glance slanted sideways, seeking the visitor, who was watching her without seeing her. This was a man, her mind declared, and she shivered in the tropical heat.

'Here's Ted coming back,' she said sharply. 'Could you defer your breakdown for a few minutes and sort out these packages? Anything with a two on it goes into the pick-up. Can your scrambled brain handle that?'

He flashed a smile at her, and fireworks exploded in her blood.

'This is not happening!' she muttered, thrusting her head back into the plane's interior. 'Attraction—and that's all it is,' she assured herself, 'could not be so capricious!'

'When you've finished your conversation with the plane fairy, we'll go over home for some lunch.' Ted's slow bushman's drawl brought her head back reluctantly out of the cramped hold. 'Young Lisa Crampton's baby's been real sick. You might be taking her and the little 'un back with you.'

Carole confirmed Ted's assumption when they met at the house.

'There's projectile vomiting and he's dehydrated. I'd say he could have a pyloric stenosis.' She smiled at Jack Fletcher as she spoke. 'More gut problems,' she said, half apologising that the condition should be his speciality but not asking for his help.

'What do you do about the dehydration?' he asked, enough interest in his voice to win Carole's confidence again.

'I've put in a slow drip, but we'll take him back with us. Lisa spoke to the doctor in Derby before she left home and knew she'd be having a trip to town. She's brought her bag.'

'Before she left home?'

Carole had walked back into the house, so Gaby was left with the question.

'The Crampton property is about eighty miles due east of here—getting out into the wild country,' she replied carelessly, her mind still battling to rationalise her totally ridiculous attraction towards this man.

'And she's been sitting out there with a child who can't keep anything down for how long?' he demanded, and she shrugged.

'Who knows? I shouldn't think it would have been for too long, because we didn't know about bringing them in before we left Derby, and if it had been an emergency someone would have flown out before this.'

'Would they?' he asked. The strange intonation in his voice slung her back into the present and she looked at him, wondering what he was really asking, and if his eyes—like the sea—might be less blue when the sky was overcast.

'Only if they knew there was a problem,' she said slowly, and nodded as if agreeing with her own statement. 'Part of the reason for poorer health standards out here is that people tend to wait and hope they might get better before they ask for treatment. Lisa would have known the clinic plane was coming, and probably decided not to call the doctor until the day it was due, thinking the situation didn't warrant an emergency flight.'

'She shouldn't have had to be the judge of that.' He was challenging her. 'If the doctors are so good at phone diagnosis, she could have been told within hours of the vomiting starting that there was a real problem.'

'It's not always that easy.' Gaby looked directly into the blue eyes that disturbed her so much, willing him to understand this very different lifestyle. 'Lisa has a two-year-old as well as Jimmy. At this time of the year her husband would be out all day, every day, shifting stock as the rains come and creeks start running. By waiting till clinic day she can bring Melissa with her, and the Egans, or one of the other families at the clinic, will care for her until Lisa can get back.'

'But the baby could have died,' he said, and she bristled at the implied criticism.

'Well, he didn't,' she retorted, 'but plenty of babies did, and still do, not only out here but in your huge cities and big fancy hospitals too. You're welcome to believe what you want, but the people who live out here have to balance a lot of factors before they make even the simplest of decisions.'

'I apologise most humbly, ma'am.' He bowed low,

sweeping off an imaginary hat. 'I'm just a poor city doctor, as you say, battling to comprehend the vastness of this country and the complexities of a service that's hard for a man like myself to believe.'

He smiled properly now, and the fireworks turned to sky rockets which erupted with frenzied whooshes through her body.

Don't 'ma'am' me, she wanted to yell, but knew her irritation was caused by her own bizarre reaction to his apology, not the Americanism. Maybe his possible nervous breakdown was contagious, she decided, and walked away from him to speak to friends who were gathered at the house.

They took off again an hour later, the plan refuelled and with Lisa, holding baby Jimmy, strapped into the spare seat. Cloud had swept across the sky while they were having lunch and the day was now so sultry that sweat ran in rivulets down Gaby's back. She looked anxiously at the lowering ceiling, and knew Jack Fletcher wouldn't be seeing a mission station on this trip.

'Be as quick as you can at Olga Creek, Carole,' she said, on the short hop between the two properties. 'Little Elvie's getting closer by the minute.'

'These pilots all get panicky with a bit of wind,' Carole complained to Jack. 'Myself, I quite like the bumpy rides—it breaks up the monotony.'

'Is flying over this incredible country really monotonous to you?' He waved his hand to display the red ridges and dark gorges beneath them.

There was such disbelief in his voice that Gaby had to smile.

'It's a job!' Carole replied, and Gaby could imagine the shrug that would have accompanied the words.

'Once you've done a few hundred clinic flights, and about the same number of emergency flights, you realise that how you get to your patients doesn't matter.'

'Carole must have done close to a thousand flights over this area,' Lisa put in. 'It's no wonder she gets bored with the form of transport.'

'And you don't feel obliged to crash-land once in a while to add a little variety to her life?'

He turned to Gaby, a wicked half-smile teasing his face into more relaxed lines.

'I did put her down on a clay pan once that wasn't as smooth as it looked from the air,' she told him, trying to ignore the quirking lips.

'Broke the wheel struts when we hit a bump and damaged one of Mike's best planes. He was *not* happy,' Carole added, chuckling at the memory.

'And once one of the other pilots landed on Gibb River Road, thinking it was a station airstrip, and met a four-wheel-drive convoy coming the other way,' Lisa told him.

Gaby listened to the talk, absorbing the unfamiliar rhythms of the man's deep, accented voice, but concentrating on the tricky approach to Olga Creek in the unpredictable wind.

'But it's a gorge! You can't land there! You'll hit the cliff!' the man said suddenly, and Gaby smiled. From his side of the plane, the clearing on the top rim of the deep chasm was invisible. It appeared far trickier than it was, because the runway was shorter than normal and the cleared space looked like a pocket handkerchief from the air.

'It's her favourite strip for showing off,' Carole told him as Gaby dropped the wheels on to the ground only feet from the edge of the cliff, and let the plane slow as it ran up the slight slope.

'Because we take off over the gorge, we don't need as much length in the runway,' she explained kindly while Jack took a steadying breath and wiped his brow with an exaggerated gesture.

'The real challenge is surviving Dave's driving down to the homestead,' Carole told him.

'I'd like to go down with him,' Lisa said quickly as they extricated themselves. 'I've spoken to Pat on the phone but haven't ever met her.'

She sounded as excited as a child on a special outing, Gaby thought, then shuddered as she remembered the cliff-hugging road.

'I stay with the plane at Olga Creek,' she said, starting the chore of unloading yet again. 'I even bring a Thermos so I can picnic up here while Carole's away.'

'Maybe I could stay with you,' Jack suggested tentatively. The meekness irritated Gaby, because she knew instinctively that he was not a meek or uncertain man. Hadn't he been goading her earlier in the day?

Was he sick? And if he was, why didn't he know? He *was* a doctor, after all!

'If Lisa's coming down it might be as well if you wait here,' Carole said. 'You'd have had to sit in the back of the utility if you wanted a lift!' She laughed at the shocked expression on his face, then added kindly, 'And we'll leave little Jimmy and you can watch his drip.'

Lisa looked dubious, but Gaby knew she would enjoy her short visit far more without the baby.

'We'll both keep an eye on him, Lisa,' she said quickly. 'I'll pull out an emergency swag and swing it like a hammock in the shade over there. They have ropes at each end and netting to protect him from the flies.' She waved a hand towards the dense scrub at the edge of the clearing. 'The clever doctor can probably improvise sufficiently well to suspend Jimmy's drip above him,' she added.

The roar of an engine heralded Dave's arrival, so Gaby took the sleeping child and handed him to the man, watching his face for a reaction.

For a moment he seemed nonplussed, then one arm tightened round the small figure, and his free hand lifted the squelchy bag of liquid and held it high to check that the tube hadn't tangled in the transfer and that the tap was still fixed in the correct position.

While Dave and Carole loaded the parcels on to the small utility, Gaby dragged out the swag and carried it across to the scrub.

'Don't stay gossiping. I want to get away as soon as I possibly can,' she called back to Carole. She hitched the rope at one end firmly round a fork in the nearest tree, then unwound the swag to find the other rope.

'Clever idea!' the man remarked, watching her work with unabashed amusement.

'Plenty of reasons to be off the ground in some of these parts,' she responded briefly, wondering why the sight of this virtual stranger cradling a baby in his arms should be affecting her so powerfully.

'Ants?' he asked, and she nodded, swinging on the second knot to make certain it was secure.

'And snakes, and water, and crocodiles, to name a few,' she said, then chuckled when she saw the look on his face.

'But hardly ever all of them at once!'

She walked over to him and lifted the baby out of

his arms, flinching slightly in response to the accidental meeting of her skin with his.

'I'll take him, if you handle the drip.' She sounded brusque, but how was she supposed to sound when standing this close to him sent her body into spasms of uncertainty?

When Jimmy was settled, she walked quickly away, heading for the edge of the precipice to look down into the dark purple slash of the gorge, as if her hovering presence could get Carole back sooner.

'Shouldn't you be watching the baby?' she asked when she heard his heavy footssteps drawing steadily nearer.

'He's so weak, poor little mite, he's drifted back to sleep.'

'Weakened by the dehydration?' Gaby asked, wondering if Lisa had been taking a risk with Jimmy's life by putting off her call to the doctor.

'More likely tired, if he's been awake all night throwing up whatever his mother has tried to put into him. His pulse is steady and his skin tone is good.'

She heard the shuffle of his movements, then he was sitting beside her.

What's bothering you? she wanted to ask, but the man was a stranger—someone she would never see again, after she delivered him back to Derby this afternoon.

'What's pyloric stenosis?' she asked instead, because Jimmy seemed the safest topic of conversation.

'It's a blockage or narrowing of the pyloric sphincter that lets food out of the stomach into the duodenum,' he told her, but the smile that hovered behind the words sent another message. 'Do you want to know what we do about it?'

I want to know why you're so uptight—so tense, even when you smile, that I can feel the vibrations coming from your body now, while we're sitting looking out over such beauty.

'I suppose so,' she said, because she somehow knew that he wasn't a man to pour out his troubles to a stranger.

'You don't really, do you?'

She turned to look at him, and received the full-blown, one hundred per cent smile.

'No,' she said, shaking her head as she smiled back at him. What I want to do is kiss you!

The thought was so shocking that she dug her fingers into the dirt and clung to the rock beneath them, fearing the world might spin out of conrol and send her toppling over the edge.

'It's a spell this ancient land is casting,' he said, so softly that she barely heard the words.

Then he leaned towards her until his lips met hers and she remembered the day—years ago, in her childhood—when the whole box of fireworks had caught fire and the expensive assortment of pinwheels and starbursts and candles had exploded as one in an array of dizzying, dazzling brilliance.

'I'll check on Jimmy!'

It was a good excuse to move away from him, but would her legs support her when she stood up, or would she go toppling over the edge and down into the gorge beneath them?

He did not reply, merely settling back on to his elbows, his face turned up to study the thickening clouds.

Jimmy slept peacefully while the swag swayed back and forth in the breeze.

I can't stand here watching a sleeping baby until the others come back she realised, and drifted back towards the plane. Retrieving the Thermos, she poured coffee for herself, looked over at the man and shook her head. If he wanted it, he could come for it.

Nursing the mug in her hands, she turned her attention to the plane. Fixing her mind firmly back into work mode, she walked around it, visually checking it with eyes trained to notice any irregularity. It was flying well, she acknowledged, wondering again what it was that Charlie Papa Bravo had been trying to tell her yesterday.

She had circled three times before the radio crackled to life, and she reached into the cockpit to acknowledge her call sign.

'It's Carole, Gaby. I'm still at Dave's. A family, touring through, has just arrived here with the twelve-year-old kid driving. It seems the father was lighting the gas stove—one of those burners on a small cylinder—at lunchtime to make tea——'

Gaby swore, crisply and fluently, knowing what was coming, and feeling an oppression not caused by the lowering weather settling round her shoulders.

'—and it exploded. He's got burns to the side of his face, shoulder and right arm. The kid helped him into the car and headed for here while Mum had hysterics in the back seat.'

'She'll need to do a total body surface area estimate,' Jack Fletcher said, lifting the radio headphone out of Gaby's hand.

He flipped the switch and spoke.

'It's Jack here, Carole. What's the TBSA affected, and are any of the wounds, particularly the chest wound, circumferential?'

Maybe he's decided he is a doctor, Gaby thought as she heard the crisp, professional voice rapping out the questions.

'I'd say fifteen to twenty per cent, Jack, and no constricting circumferential. I've covered them with a dry, sterile dressing, given him three milligrams of morphine intravenously and started a saline drip.'

'Do you want me to head down the track and meet you?'

'No, Jack. I'm staying. You'd be more use if the fellow decides to get worse on the plane, and I know the way back to Derby by road——'

'Are you sure, Carole? I'd be happy to give up my seat,' he broke in, but Gaby shook her head at him, knowing that Carole's decision was the most sensible solution. She took the headset from him as Carole finished,

'Quite sure, thanks. I'm sending my bag back in the ute with Dave and the patient. Good luck.'

'It's Gaby, Carole. If you're driving out, do you know which rivers are threatening and that the latest weather forecast shows Elvie still heading for the coast but on a south-easterly course now?'

'I've talked to Dave and he'll phone ahead and let people know I'm coming through. The wife's not much use. She's in no state to be left alone and the twelve-year-old's likely to go into delayed shock any minute. He's a spunky kid but he's done enough for one day. I can't let them drive out on their own. Phone my family and tell them I'll be home for Christmas,' she joked, but Gaby grew more uneasy by the moment. With two drivers, the ground party could be back in Derby by morning, but if the injured man's wife didn't or couldn't drive Carole would have to camp out. If the cyclone continued on its present track, it could be a long, wet trip.

She reactivated the radio, calling Olga Creek.

'Why don't you stay there, and I'll come back for you all in the morning?' she suggested, and heard Carole's chuckle.

'There are five kids, Gaby,' she explained, 'and if the weather closes in and we can't get out I don't think Dave and his missus would thank you.'

Little devils, are they? Gaby thought, but, knowing that they might all be clustered around the radio, she didn't say it.

'OK, Carole,' she agreed, then closed down as she heard a motor roaring as it came up from the gorge.

'Let's get organised,' she told Jack. 'If you take Jimmy, I'll roll the swag and pack the plane. You can have a few minutes to check on the patient when he gets here, then we're off.'

The wind was gusting now, and she was worried about the contrary bursts that flung themselves across the runway. The concern quickened her steps towards the shelter of the trees and made her fingers fumble as she picked up the still sleeping baby and handed him to the man who had followed her.

'What's bothering you?' he asked, and she looked at him in amazement as he asked the question she'd left unasked earlier.

You, her eyes replied as they met his, a sudden sadness forcing its way through the tumult of anxiety inside her mind.

'I don't know,' she lied, and turned away to take down the swag and roll it up carefully.

'How long will the flight back to Derby take?' he

asked, hovering over her as he rocked the baby back and forth in his arms.

'An hour and a half, or maybe a little longer.'

'Then I'll draw up a second pain-killer for the patient before we leave here, in case he gets restless on the flight. If you put Lisa and the baby in the front, I'll sit beside him and keep an eye on him.'

'You're reacting like a doctor,' she pointed out, straightening from her task and looking up into his face.

'I reckon I must be one, then,' he said, and smiled at her.

For the first time she saw what he must have looked like when he was younger. Or when he was happier? Had whatever doubts he'd been fighting etched the lines into his face, or did the unhappiness she had sensed in him come from his home life? His marriage?

The utility rattled to a halt by the plane before she could question why the thought of his marriage caused her physical pain. Her mind switched back to business as she prepared to get away from this place and return to base as quickly as she could.

Lisa leapt from the back of the vehicle and lifted out three parcels that were to go to Derby before retrieving her son from Jack. Dave helped Jack lift the wounded man across to the plane, and together they heaved him up into a seat.

Gaby shut her mind to the groans of pain, knowing that her job was to get him to specialist care and nothing more. She stacked the gear away, passing Carole's bag to Jack and waiting while he checked what it held.

'Do you need anything from the cool-box?'

He looked up and shook his head, but as he did he

smiled again, and she forgot everything but the blueness of his eyes and the new, excited spark of life in her veins.

'Will you hold Jimmy while I get in then pass him through to me?' Lisa asked, bringing her back to the real world once again.

She took the baby and hugged him tight, too bamboozled by what was happening to her to think straight.

'OK, I'm all set,' Jack announced, taking his seat beside his unexpected patient while Lisa settled Jimmy on her lap.

Gaby closed the door, and walked around to climb into the cockpit.

Concentrate on flying until we get home, she ordered herself. In two hours from now you can think about other things—if there are other things to be considered!

The muddled internal monologue continued while she did her pre-flight instrument checks, but it turned to admonition when she taxied down the slight slope and found part of her mind still lurking on married men and blue eyes. Turning parallel to the gorge, she started the ascent, rising steadily towards clouds that were much lower than before.

She radioed her departure and arrival times, her mind now fully focused on her work, and, lifting to fifteen hundred feet, turned the little plane and headed for home. The rain was starting now, as the clouds moved over the heated land, lifted higher and dropped their burden. It came in from the coast like a grey sheet of muslin, blotting out all colour and reducing familiar landmarks to indistinct blurs.

Clouds and rain combined to bring an early dusk, and the winds shook and rattled the frail craft as it beat back towards Derby. Gaby needed total concentration to hold it steady, while keeping a close watch on the instrument panel, checking outside, then back to the panel, alert for any sign that external stresses might be doing some damage.

Intent on her job, she heard Jack speak, but he had repeated the words twice before they registered.

'—cardiac arrest, and I can't do anything here. Can we go back, or land somewhere else?'

He sounded desperate. Gaby's mind raced through possible solutions, sparing only a fleeting second of regret for not having taken Fred's advice and flown a Kingair today.

'It's too dark to land on the short strip at Olga Creek, so there's no point in turning back.'

She turned west into the worsening weather. As a child she had often flown to the coast with her father to fish, landing on a deserted airstrip built during the war more than fifty years ago. It was due west from Teralga which was due east from Olga Creek.

She checked her watch. They had been flying south for ten minutes. Once she found the coast—and surely it would be the one recognisable feature in the rain?— the airstrip should be ten minutes to the north, just past the wide stretch of Stratton Sound.

'I'll be fifteen minutes,' she told Jack, carefully watching her compass as she turned to the new heading.

'He's giving mouth to mouth,' Lisa informed her. 'The fellow looks grey—real sick!'

Gaby shuddered, then reached for the radio, calling back to base. Wild static greeted her, and her fingers spun the two knobs back and forth, seeking a clear signal.

There was no response and she realised, with a

stomach-turning dread, that the usual intermitten chatter from the machine had been missing since they'd taken off from Olga Creek.

Had it been missing earlier? She'd spoken to Olga Creek but not to base since she left Windaroo. Her mind skittered towards panic, but she calmed herself and transmitted her message.

'Emergency on board, am heading for old wartime airstrip south of Kalumburu. Radio not receiving so would anyone hearing this message please advise RFDS base Derby?' She repeated it on three different frequencies, her watchful gaze flicking from the panel to the windows then back again. At least the coastline was where it should be, she realised with relief, but the fast-falling darkness frightened her. Ahead she could see a broad cleared space, and the whitish strip of the runway. She uttered a silent prayer of thanks to the father who had brought her here so often.

She descended slowly, circling once to get her bearings, while the wind shook and rattled at the plane's fabric.

'I'm going to do a tight left-hand circuit above the strip before I come in to land,' she told Lisa. 'Look out your window and see if you can see any big objects we might hit or any holes I should avoid.'

She steadied the stick, levelling out about five hundred feet above the darker southern approach to the strip. Then the blackness beneath them moved, and, as she watched, it seemed to stream off into the trees at one side of the runway.

'Wild donkeys,' Lisa told her. 'They must make their beds there for the warmth.'

'As long as they haven't been using it long enough

to make a wallow in the middle of it,' Gaby replied through gritted teeth.

She had to land if the man was to be treated properly and she had to land carefully if she wanted to be certain of taking off again when he has been stabilised.

She lifted up and around, coming back in as slowly as she dared, nursing the stick in fingers that shook with tension. The wheels touched, skidded slightly, hopped then steadied, and she braked as firmly as she dared on the wet surface, not willing to count on the entire runway being trouble-free.

The plane slowed to a walk, and she applied more brake, then felt the backward thrust and heard the snap before they all lurched forward and the plane tipped sickeningly on to one wing.

It wasn't a donkey-wallow, but an old forty-four-gallon drum, painted white and invisible on the wet surface of the runway. But she didn't know that until later.

CHAPTER FOUR

'Is there a risk of fire?'

Jack asked the question calmly, his voice lifting above the whimpering of the child and Lisa's panicky gasps.

'No!' Gaby assured him, hoping she sounded equally calm. 'Lisa, I want you and Jimmy to stay where you are for the moment.'

She gripped the woman's arm, shaking her slightly to emphasise the suggestion. Lisa nodded, and Gaby turned to Jack.

'What do you need first?'

'Oxygen,' he said, lifting his head from his almost leisured supplementation of the man's breathing. 'And enough space to lay him flat and make sure I've got a clear airway until I can stabilise him.'

She sat and thought for a moment.

'The swag is on top of the luggage but it will be hard to get at the hatch. I'll open the door on this side, scramble out, and try to reach in for it. Once I've got it on the ground, we should be able to ease the chap out and on to it, and you can keep working on him while I get the emergency resuscitation kit out.'

Jack muttered what seemed like agreement to these plans, and Gaby wondered if he realised it wasn't going to be as easy as she had made it sound.

She forced open her door and slid out into the rain. Bending to crawl under the slanting wing, she realised that at least there was a reasonably dry space under the plane.

She reached in behind the back seats and retrieved the swag, blessing the thick outer covering of oilskin that would keep the inner cocoon dry.

'Don't open it right out, Gaby,' Jack warned her as she dragged it past the unconscious passenger. 'We need to keep the blankets inside as dry as possible if we want to warm him later.'

She nodded, too overwhelmingly glad that he was there to speak.

Spreading it on the ground, she realised that Jack had somehow opened his door— which pointed up towards the sky—and joined her beneath the wing. He put his arms around the man's body, sliding him up and out of the seat. To share the weight, Gaby grabbed at his legs as they came free.

Not plastic muscles after all! The transitory thought stunned her. The mind she thought was concentrating on their plight had wandered off again!

They lowered the man and she clambered over him and back into the plane, shifting parcels on to the spare seat until she came to the blue Oxyvac box.

'What else?' she asked as she pushed it through the door to Jack.

'Carole's bag which is under the seat,' he said, his hands moving swiftly to attach a tube and mask to the oxygen bottle, 'and a torch. There should be lidocaine in the bag. I might need it if he shows signs of tachycardia—rapid heartbeats—to regulate the rhythm. I'll need more morphine as well, but the shot Carole gave him earlier should still be holding the worst of his pain at bay.'

She found Carole's bag and reached into the front

seat for her torch. Clutching them both on her knee, she sat for a moment and thought about their position.

The rain beat steadily down now, reminding her that shelter had to be her first priority. There was a sandstone cave, hollowed out by wind and weather into a long, curving tunnel that ran down towards the sea. Her father's father had camped there as a child, then her father and herself. It was part of her most precious memories.

Steadied by the thought, she swung back into action, passing the medical equipment down to Jack before delving into the back compartment again.

'Here's a small tarpaulin, Lisa,' she said, thrusting the bulky parcel through between the seats. 'I'll take Jimmy and you climb over here and get out under the wing. Pull the tarp over your head and work out how you can hold it and the baby before I pass him out to you.'

'Will do, Gaby,' Lisa said, responding to the order with a half-snapped salute.

Gaby grinned at her, thanking heaven the young woman hadn't gone to pieces in the crisis.

'I'll hop out after you've taken Jimmy and lead you across to shelter. If you can make him comfortable on the tarp, you might scout around for firewood when you get there. No one's going to come and take us home tonight.'

Did she sound light-hearted enough to hide her fear?

'Pass me my bag, I'll carry that,' Lisa suggested, but Gaby shook her head.

'It's blowing a gale out there. You'll be flat out getting across to shelter safely and keeping both of you as dry as possible. I'll bring your bag, then come back to help Jack with his patient.'

Because I got you into this mess, she added in her head as a futile argument about choices began to beat in her brain.

'His name's Bernie,' Lisa said as she passed the fractious child back between the seats.

Gaby looked down at Jimmy and wondered if Lisa had bumped her head when they'd stopped so abruptly.

'The man with the burns!' Lisa explained, scrambling across the gap between the seats then out through the door. 'OK,' she called, and her arms reached out from beneath a thick knot of tarpaulin.

Gaby handed her the baby, then grabbed Lisa's bag and the emergency pack that all RFDS planes carried and extricated herself with difficulty. She landed on the ground beside Jack, who was carefully sorting through the bottles and vials in Carole's bag.

What if he's not a doctor? The thought sprang from nowhere in her head, but she refused to contemplate such a macabre chance. Surely someone had checked that out before they'd offered him an observer's seat on the flight?

'I'm taking Lisa to shelter. I'll be back shortly,' she told him.

It took her a minute to get her bearings, then her feet led her unerringly off the tarmac and through the scrabbly, wind-swept trees to the slight depression she remembered. It was there that the first part of the ridge that formed the cave had collapsed centuries earlier.

Pushing through the thicker bushes in the sheltered hollow, she cursed the fact that she had not brought the torch, then realised that the emergency pack should have one.

'Squat down for a minute with your back to the wind,' she told Lisa.

Opening the box, she felt for what she wanted, finding the smooth cylinder within seconds. The torch showed her the little tomahawk, and she picked it out, closed the box and shone the torch towards where she thought the entrance to the cave would be. It illuminated the wet green leaves of a black wattle and she smiled. The little tree refused to die, no matter how many times visiting fishermen cut it back to get into the shelter behind it.

'Could you hold the torch for me?' she asked Lisa, waving the circle of light towards the tree. 'I need to get a few branches off that.'

Five minutes later she was ushering the woman and child into the warm, dry interior, sweeping the torch around in search of snakes, centipedes or other unwelcome visitors.

'You're a genius,' Lisa told her, eyeing the large empty space with wonder.

Sure! Gaby's mind responded. A genius who risked the lives of four other people to possibly save the life of one. A genius who reacted amutomatically to an order from someone who isn't even part of the service!

'A fire would be good,' she reminded Lisa. 'You keep the torch. You'll find matches and fire-starters in the emergency pack. I'm off.'

She left the shelter reluctantly, although she was already so wet that she couldn't possibly get any wetter.

'We'll need Lisa's help to carry him,' Jack said when she slumped down under the wing beside him.

'We need Lisa dry and happy, which means she stays with Jimmy,' Gaby contradicted him. 'You'd be surprised how strong RFDS pilots have to be.'

She could not see his face in the darkness but knew he was looking at her.

'I've another tarpaulin in the plane. I'll get it and we can cover him with that to keep him dry. You figure out how we can keep a drip and an oxygen bottle and mask in place while we carry him.'

She climbed back into the cabin, feeling coldness creep under her skin as she moved away from Jack.

It was the stuff of nightmares, she decided a little later. She staggered under the combined weight of swag and man, yet gritted her teeth and forced her legs to keep moving and her hands to retain their grip on the makeshift stretcher. A flickering light from the mouth of the cave told her Lisa had found some wood, but it wasn't getting any closer.

'Ten more steps,' Jack urged. 'That's all, Gaby. You can do it.'

Her feet slipped on the incline and she staggered, then steadied, stumbling towards the welcoming glow.

Lisa's hands reached out and tucked around hers. She felt the weight lessen slightly as together they brought the man into the shelter and lowered him to the ground.

Jack lifted the covering canvas and began to settle Bernie more comfortably.

'I'll go back and get the bag,' he said, but Gaby shook her head.

'You've got two patients to attend,' she told him almost curtly. 'I'll get the bag and the rest of the stuff from the plane.' She turned and walked away, back out into the rain.

There was another swag, she knew that much, having packed and unpacked it often enough today. And she knew where the newly donated emergency rations were—and water.

Turning her face up into the deluge, she laughed.

All small planes carried water. Exactly what you needed on the edge of a cyclone!

The wind was strengthening, and the trained part of her brain wondered about the sense or otherwise of tying down the plane. The wheel was too badly bent to take off again, but if the winds increased and it was flung about on the tarmac, would it become unsalvageable?

She carried Carole's bag and the second swag back first, knowing that Lisa would be able to make Jimmy more comfortable in the soft, inner folds. If Jimmy didn't need her, Lisa might volunteer to be cook—if cook was a word you could apply to dried food.

'Don't go back out there!' Jack spoke so sharply that she swung round at the edge of the circle of light.

'One more trip,' she told him, trying hard to smile through the rivulets of water running down her face. 'Food,' she added tiredly, unable to spare the energy for more words.

'I'll go,' he muttered and she heard a muffled anger in his voice.

'You'll stay right here,' she told him. 'It's pitch-black outside and the one thing I don't need is a lost American stumbling around in the bush.'

She received a thunderous scowl in reply and trudged out into the wet night.

The plane was rocking, its panels moaning as they moved against each other, protesting against the unnatural angle and the onslaught of the wind.

'I'll come back and tie you down,' she promised as she left with the last of the supplies they would require to see them comfortably through the night.

'There should be everything you need including a

small, concentrated fuel stove in here,' she told Lisa, who was watching Jack examine Jimmy.

She dropped the pack, picked up the tomahawk and headed back out before anyone could argue with her. Common sense told her that tying down the plane was stupid, but instinct told her she should do it, and instinct had taken over when she'd realised that the little group's survival might depend on her.

Rain pelted against her skin like stones and she shivered as the wind forced her feet swiftly across the ground towards the aircraft.

The plane carried steel stakes and ropes, and she thanked the fates that the old concrete offered little resistance as she belted the stakes into the ground. Securing the ropes to the tie-down points on the plane, she dragged back on them with all her weight before fastening them to the pegs. Once they were secured, she sat down on the runway in the sheltered lee side and tried to think through their situation.

First, there was the radio. Unless this rain was the edge of a violent electrical storm that had disrupted the airwaves, then there was a fault in her radio or in the plane's electrical system.

She thought about a storm and eliminated it. Even at one thousand feet, she would have seen the evidence of it in lightning flashes somewhere on the horizon.

An electric fault? Her instruments had been working when she'd turned towards the coast. They had been working when she'd watched her approach and fly-through on the altimeter.

It had to be the radio!

Damn! I thought it was the plane—didn't consider the radio! she scolded herself, remembering her insist-

ence that Fred check and re-check the chartered plane
before they left Broome.

What now? she asked herself. Weariness swept over
her, and she clambered up and slid back into the
cockpit. Turning on the ignition, she tried the radio
again, but no echo of a voice came through the broken
crackling confusion.

'This is Charlie Papa Bravo,' she said carefully. It
wouldn't do for any chance listener to hear the despair
in her voice. 'We are on the ground, and have food
and safe shelter. One wheel bent so couldn't take off
even if the weather eases. Burns patient suffered heart
attack in air. Visiting doctor treating him and child. No
other injuries or concerns.'

Again and again she repeated the message, yelling
against the noise of wind and rain, trying every possible
channel. How many times had a radio ham picked up
a message from someone in distress? Would it happen
tonight? Would someone hear and pass on the news
that they were safe?

The thought of her family's anxiety was like a
crushing weight she would have done anything to
alleviate.

Anything?

As she bent her head into the lashing force of the
rain and forced her way back towards the cave, she
concentrated fiercely. If her mother's intuitive sense
could pick up premonitions of danger, surely she could
receive good news as well?

'I'm safe, Mum! Safe! Safe! Safe!' she yelled into the
elemental force of wind and rain and blackness, caper-
ing like a madman through the bush towards the cave.

'We're very glad to hear it,' a deep voice replied,
and she was caught in Jack's arms and pulled under the

dubious shelter of the tarp he held above his head. He pressed her tightly against his chest for a moment, the drenching wetness running down her face and shoulders and pooling between them.

'I—I thought I told you to stay in the cave,' she stuttered, battling an urge to laugh and cry at the same time.

'I couldn't,' he said simply, squeezing her closer to his solidity and warmth. 'But I wasn't about to get lost.'

His voice had lightened and she knew he was smiling, although the darkness was too dense for her to see his face.

'I found a ball of string and tied one end to the battered little bush at the entrance.' There was a momentary silence, before he added in a voice that held despair instead of laughter, 'I've come all this way, but could only have gone as far as a ball of string to find you again.'

She shivered suddenly and uncontrollably. Surely she had enough problems without this man making statements that made no sense at all, yet made her feel sad and glad at the same time?

His cheek was resting against her wet hair and warmth was seeping from his body into hers.

'Come inside and get dry,' he murmured, turning her so that his arm was about her shoulders and guiding her stumbling footsteps back towards the cave.

Inside, the fury of the weather dulled to a muted, keening moan as the wind swept across the seaward end of the cavern, playing on the emptiness like a performer's breath on an instrument. The fire crackled brightly, and Lisa's anxious face turned towards her.

'I'm sorry I was so long. I was sending a message out

to let everyone know we were all safe.' She crossed her fingers behind her back. Her message might have got through, but, if it hadn't, why burden Lisa with another problem?

'I was worried about Mark worrying,' Lisa told her with a cheerful smile. 'Now we can relax and pretend we're on a camping holiday until someone comes in to get us out.'

Gaby welcomed the sensible wait-and-see attitude of the bush. She moved closer to the fire, pulling her wet shirt away from her skin and flapping it towards the flames.

'If the rain is the beginning of Cyclone Elvie, it could be a few days before a plane can fly in,' she warned. 'You might check through those food reserves and sort them into daily parcels so we've something left for later if the low hangs around for a while.'

'I'll do it now,' Lisa told her, seemingly pleased to have a job to occupy her time.

Now Gabby turned towards the dark shadows at the edge of the cave where Jack was bent over Jimmy.

'How will your patients handle a few days here?' she asked quietly, then watched him straighten and walk towards her.

'Jimmy will be fine. There's sugar, salt and even baking soda in the emergency rations. If we run out of Ringer's lactate or I need it for Bernie we can boil water to purify it and I can make up a sustaining drip to keep him hydrated.'

'And Bernie?' she asked, turning to look at the man who lay so still.

'He's stable at the moment. There's enough morphine in the bag to keep the pain at bay.'

He frowned and rubbed his fingers across his fore-head in a way that made her heart ache.

'The first problem with burns patients is fluid loss as fluid is drawn from the blood and tissues. This puts the patient at risk of kidney failure and stomach ulceration, among other things.'

'But if Carole started him straight away on a drip. . .?' She hesitated, wishing she had more medical knowledge.

'We should be able to keep the worst of the complications at bay,' he told her gently. 'Isotonic solutions like saline or Ringer's, which has a good electrolyte concentration, are fine for the first twenty-four hours, but after that we've got to start adding calories to his diet to avoid muscle wastage as the body converts the protein stored in the muscles to glucose to use in its fight against the injury.'

Gaby shuddered. It seemed far too complicated to work out while caught by a cyclone in a cave on the edge of nowhere.

'And can you make up a solution to provide what he needs out of the emergency rations?' she asked as lightly as she could.

'If I have to,' he told her seriously, then smiled. 'But once I've got him stabilised I'd prefer to see him eating or at least being fed through his stomach. Intravenous calorie supplementation is not the best!'

'Speaking of eating, shall we?' Lisa called to them, and Gaby turned towards her with relief. Eating might blot out the nagging questions edging back into her mind.

'I'm sorry to have landed you into this predicament,' she murmured as they walked together towards the fire, 'and in a plane that isn't fully equipped.'

'Carole's bag is full of wonders,' he assured her, his voice so free from concern that she peered suspiciously at him.

'You're enjoying this!'

A half-smile fluttered then stuck.

'Not really,' he protested unconvincingly. 'Any doctor would prefer to have his patients in a hospital with every facility at hand, but this does present certain challenges!'

'There are two sets of eating implements snapped together like Swiss army knives,' Lisa announced as they sat down near the fire. 'I'll use the measuring spoon out of Jimmy's formula tin and——'

'You've got milk formula with you?' Jack demanded, reaching out to grasp Lisa's arm in his excitement.

'Of course,' she replied, startled by his reaction. 'Formula and boiled water and some tins of baby apple purée. I didn't know what might happen on the trip to Windaroo, especially in the wet, and, although he had been throwing up all that I gave him, I knew I had to keep trying to get something into him.'

'Blessed girl!' Jack sighed, shaking his head and smiling broadly at the same time.

Gaby felt a spurt of sadness that the glowing smile wasn't for her, but as Lisa put a pannikin of warm food into her hands she forgot everything but her sudden hunger.

Silence fell while they all attacked the food, the single pannikin passing from one pair of hands to the next, all taking a spoonful before passing it on.

'There's a coil of tubing in Carole's bag,' Jack said, lying back on his elbows when the strange meal was finished. 'I reckon I can rig up a naso-gastric feeding tube for Bernie, and with Jimmy's formula, maybe double strength, we'll keep him going.'

Lisa left the fire to pick up the baby, and Gaby wondered if she would be willing to give up the formula for the injured man. The young mother carried Jimmy back into the warm circle of light, the precious bag dangling from her fingers.

'He's got a wet nappy for the first time in twenty-four hours,' she announced with a certain amount of pride. 'But he's grizzly and unsettled.'

She put him down to change his nappy, handing Gaby the half-empty fluid bag to hold while she attended to him.

'Wouldn't his stomach be telling him he's hungry although he's on the drip?' Gaby asked Jack, concerned for the fretful infant.

'It shouldn't be, but his sucking instinct would still be in operation. Does he have a pacifier?'

'What on earth's a pacifier?' Lisa asked, then chuckled as she saw the man put his thumb into his mouth and curl his forefinger round his nose in an exact parody of a child thumb-sucking.

'A dummy!' she cried. 'I did have one, because Melissa liked one, but Jimmy has never fancied it much.'

She rifled through the capacious bag and produced a small plastic container.

'There are sterilising tablets in Carole's bag. I'll dissolve one in water and dunk it in that for a few minutes before you give it to him, just to be on the safe side,' Jack told her as he stood up and took it from her hand. 'Cuddling him when he's awake will also help.'

He walked away and Gaby watched Lisa bend over

the baby, a poignant longing stirring to life deep within her.

When Jack returned, he examined the little boy carefully.

'I'll take him off the drip now. That way he can sleep with you in the second swag and you won't both get tangled up in the tube. If you wake during the night, use the torch and check his fontanelle, and his feet. If he's becoming dehydrated the slight depression there will become sunken——' he touched his finger to the little skull '—and the creases in his feet will deepen.'

Lisa nodded her understanding, accepting the responsiblity for monitoring her child with a gravity that belied her youth.

'And what about Bernie?' she asked. 'Should we take turns watching him? Could you tell us what to look for? You can't sit up with him all night.'

He smiled at her again.

'You've got your patient. Gaby and I will look after Bernie.'

Now Gaby was included in the smile, but it wasn't the same. She wanted a special smile—for herself alone, she thought fractiously.

He sat down beside her, but she refused to turn and look at him, staring instead into the glowing coals of the dying fire.

'Bernie is stable at the moment. I've cut back on the percentage of oxygen he's breathing and he hasn't shown any adverse reaction to the reduction. He's heavily sedated, and should stay that way all night, but there are two things we have to do.'

He was speaking directly to Gaby, but loudly enough for Lisa to hear and follow what he was saying.

'We have to measure his fluid input and output as

best we can, because an excess of fluid could be as bad as too little. It could result in hypervolemia—an increase in the volume of circulating blood. When this first lot of fluid has gone into him, I'm going to put in a catheter. . .' he paused, as if to give them time to ask a question, but both the women remained silent '. . .and drain it back into the fluid bag, using the same tube.'

Gaby shuddered, wondering what would have happened if Jack had not been with them.

I'd have flown on to Derby, and Bernie would probably have died without my knowing it, she realised.

'I'm also putting antibiotics into the drip to ward off infection, and will add regular morphine to keep the pain at bay. I'm writing down everything I'm doing in a notebook I found in Carole's bag.'

A fear as cold as death itself swept over Gaby.

'Why are you telling us all of this? Why are you writing it down?' she whispered. 'You'll be looking after him! We don't need to know!'

Silence answered her—pricklingly uncomfortable—a prelude to an unnameable terror.

'I haven't worked for four months,' he said at last, and his voice was deep and grave and full of agony. 'Before that, I was a specialist in gastroenterology at a well-known teaching hospital in Boston—top of my field, respected, a career doctor with everything going my way.'

The strained hush that greeted his statement was broken by little whiffling noises from Jimmy as he settled the pacifier more comfortably in his mouth.

'Four months, three weeks and four days ago I passed out while carrying out a simple endoscopy procedure. My head nurse took over, no damage was done to the patient, and I put it down to a virus, over-tiredness or something similar.'

Gaby reached out to touch him, then drew back the fingers that wanted to offer sympathy, but Lisa's hand moved, and Gaby saw it settle on Jack's shoulder, kneading at his bones in silent compassion.

'When it happened twice more, and none of my fellow specialists or their advanced tests could find a reason for it, I had to conclude that maybe I was suffering from a stress-related illness. I knew I couldn't continue to practise. It was sheer luck I hadn't punc-tured my patient's stomach when I fell the first time. I packed my bags, and found an old school atlas. The furthest I could get away from Boston and still be in an English-speaking country was Broome.'

Gaby's heart had contracted bit by bit with every word he uttered. Now it felt like a tiny marble, cold and hard and extremely painful.

'So we know what to do for Bernie if you pass out,' the ever practical Lisa responded. 'But what do we do for you?'

'Is that all you want to know?' Jack asked, the amazement in his voice so patent that Lisa laughed.

'Of course!' she told him. 'Gaby and I are relying on you to pull our patients through this little adventure, so looking after you should be our first consideration, shouldn't it, Gaby?'

Gaby managed a strangled grunt that she hoped sounded like agreement. She had noticed the lines in his face the first time she'd looked at him and her heart had reacted sympathetically. Now his pain had been transferred to her so totally, she could barely breathe.

He's a stranger, her head shouted, but her heart

continued to ache for the loss and loneliness that his words had imparted.

'As long as I don't hit my head on anything and bleed to death, I should pull out of it within a few seconds,' he said brusquely. 'Well, so far, whenever it's happened, I have.'

'But if you've been holidaying, the stress must be easing. It mightn't happen again,' Lisa argued, but Gaby knew the assumption was wrong. The knowing that it happened and not knowing why would be more stressful to this man than everyday work.

'It's happened since I've been in Broome,' he stated flatly, then stood up and moved away from them, striding into the darkness beyond the firelight. Gaby wondered if he regretted confiding in them, or if the anger she could now feel emanating from his disappearing back was something else.

The moaning seemed to deepen, echoing eerily around them as she leant towards the fire, not needing its warmth but seeking solace from it.

'Tough luck for him, isn't it?' Lisa remarked when the wailing noise needed to be blotted out with speech. She looked down at Jimmy, asleep in her arms. 'I think it's bedtime for us. Would you like to share the swag?'

'No way!' Gaby told her. 'You make Jimmy comfortable. There are the two tarpaulins that Jack and I can have. It sounds as if only one of us will be sleeping at a time anyway. I'll wait till he comes back and tells me what to watch for, then sort out who'll take the first shift.'

Goodnight, then,' Lisa murmured, moving towards her own shadowy spot by the wall of the cave.

Gaby closed her eyes. Spirit figures seemed to hover

around her, like the dancing shadows that the fitful
flames cast on the walls. Was it the cave, this ancient
shelter, that was making her so super-sensitive to Jack
Fletcher?

CHAPTER FIVE

GABY saw him emerge from the darkness, a blacker shadow that became a person as he drew closer to the light of the dying fire. He squatted down and dropped a pile of short thick pieces of wood beside it, feeding on one or two.

'Comforting things, fires, aren't they?' he said quietly. 'Do you think it's a hangover from some primitive memory when our ancestors kept them burning all night to keep wild animals at bay?'

'Or the fact that they provide light and we have less fear of things we can see?' Gaby asked.

He looked up, and his eyes, black in the shadows, met hers with a piercing intensity.

'But what would you know of fear, Gaby?' he asked, his voice deep and low, etched to a grave density by the emotion that still hung in the charged atmosphere. 'You're a child of love and light and laughter, a woman on whom the gods must surely smile! Your beauty alone would be a passport to everything good in life, for who could look at you and not be changed?'

His own smile flickered across his lips but didn't settle there, and its disappearance left his face dark and broodingly still.

'I'm fearful now,' she whispered. 'But not of the dark or the cyclone or wild animals or shadows.'

I feel your fear, she would have liked to add, but was too disturbed by what she felt to voice it.

He shook his head, as if he understood what she was

saying and not saying, but refused to acknowledge or respond to it.

'Are your clothes still wet?' he asked, adding more sticks to the fire.

'A bit damp, that's all,' she muttered, embarrassed and confused. He had paid her the kind of compliment that hinted at something beyond mere friendly concern, then rejected her plea for help in understanding what was happening between them. Now he was nagging about her wet clothes.

'Take them off, Gaby. You can have my shirt.'

It was an order she was unable to obey. She watched, mesmerised, as he stripped off his pale blue shirt studying the muscles that rippled in the firelight, and the skin that shone gold where the leaping reflections touched it.

'Poor kid! You've just about had it, haven't you?'

He came closer. Knelt beside her. His bare torso filled her vision and stilled her breathing.

'You've had a big day, little one,' he said soothingly, 'and brought us all safely to shelter. Now slip your wet clothes off and put this on, and I'll make a bed for you.' He handed her the shirt, still warm from his body, smelling faintly of the cologne she'd sniffed an eternity ago in the warm dawn air of Broome, then moved away. His voice was so gentle, so persuasive that she was tempted to float away on it into a long and dreamless sleep.

Yet it wasn't the promise of sleep she wanted from this man. Her body told her that. Nor did she want to be a 'little one' or a 'poor kid' to him. She rubbed her cheek against the blue material while her thoughts drifted along unfamiliar paths.

Earlier today he'd kissed her, hadn't he? And had it been the kind of kiss you'd give a child?

Now he was back, dropping down to his knees beside her, and she turned to look at him, all the questions in her dark eyes as they looked up into the blueness of his.

'No, Gaby!' His voice, hoarse and smoky, rasped across her heart, the rejection imprinting itself like a fiery brand. 'I'll help you change,' he added, the words trembling nearly as much as the fingers that reached out to undo the buttons down the front of her uniform shirt.

Of course he said no, her mind yelled. He's a married man, a stranger, passing through your life like a cloud across the sky. The eerie moaning of the wind swirled through her—the sound of loneliness.

His fingers, clumsily slow, brushed against her skin, and her body leaned into his touch, arching towards him, burning with a need she had never before experienced.

He was nearly finished! An agitated sense of loss swept over her, and her body shook as he peeled back the shirt and slid it from her shoulders and down her arms.

His breath was hissing out between his teeth, and his gaze, after one burning sweep across her creamy skin and lace-clad breasts, came up to meet hers, a reluctant head-shake reinforcing the no he'd said earlier, but the blue eyes passed a contradictory message.

Then his face seemed to contract and darken. He lifted the shirt out of her nerveless fingers and wrapped it round her shoulders, his hands biting through the fabric as they dug, for an infinitesimal moment, into her flesh.

'Don't expect me to put it on for you,' he muttered harsly. 'Flesh and blood can only stand so much!'

He seemed to push her away—a physical rejection—yet he was the one who moved, standing up and hovering above her uncertainly, before striding back towards the patient who lay so heavily sedated in the shadows.

Gaby waited, although she knew he wasn't going to come back, then thrust her arms into the sleeves of his shirt and knelt to undo her skirt and slip it down to her knees, buttoning the borrowed garment so that it satisfied modesty.

She stood up and pulled off her skirt then spread both shirt and skirt to dry beside the fire. Slowly, as if testing her weight on each step, she walked back to the man and his patient.

'What do you want me to do for him during the night?' she asked, pleased with the control that held her voice steady.

She felt him turn towards her, then his hand reached out and touched her bare leg.

He's feeling to see if I'm chilled after sitting around in damp clothes, she told herself, yet knew that there was a muted appeal, and desperation, in that light touch of skin on skin. He's reaching out to anchor himself, some strange insight told her, and she stood completely still, not wanting to break the fragile moment.

'I'll wake you and tell you if I need you,' he murmured. 'I think he should sleep right through the night. I'll sleep here beside him and will hear him if he stirs.'

Again her body tilted forward, an unspoken, involuntary plea to be allowed to share his bed that startled Gaby back to reality.

'I've folded the second tarp over some dry grass I found near the far entrance to the cave. You settle down on that and get what sleep you can.'

She hesitated, looking down on to the top of his dark head, so close that she could have run her fingers through his hair, or kneaded his shoulder as Lisa had earlier.

'Doctor's orders, Gaby.'

The cool, controlled voice reminded her that he didn't want whatever it was she felt towards him, and she walked away, settling on to the rough canvas with a firm conviction that she wouldn't sleep.

She woke to a cacophony of noise. The moaning had intensified, and a wild whistling and threshing added to it, as if some enormous animal rolled and writhed in pain above them.

'This one's not going to turn away from the coast,' she muttered to herself, and stood up as quietly as she could from her rustling makeshift bed.

'The cyclone's closer, isn't it?'

Had he been watching her, that he spoke as soon as she stood up?

'I'd say so,' she said, but she was so distracted by the initimacy of the man's unseen body sharing the noisy darkness with her that the words were almost inaudible. 'If you don't need the torch, I'd like to walk down to the seaward end of the cave. I seem to remember it being well up above the high-water mark, but we'd look silly sitting in here with waves washing over us.'

'Bernie is comfortable, so I'll come with you.' His voice was pitched low enough to reach her but not disturb the others. 'Do you get tidal surges with cyclones?'

He snapped on the torch, shining the light into a pool at her feet, then stepped towards her and took her hand, so that they could walk together where the light shone.

'Not tidal surges exactly,' she croaked, so disturbed by this man's touch that her body was going haywire, 'but the tides here have a rise and fall of up to forty feet. If the wind sweeps in, building up mountainous seas behind a full tide, then the water will wash much higher than normal.'

Even in her own ears the explanation sounded confused, but how could she think logically when his skin was burning against hers, lighting every nerve-ending in her body to a frenzied longing that terrified her with its intensity?

She stumbled on the uneven surface and slipped against him, but he steadied her then moved away, still holding tightly to her hand but now allowing her the comfort of his body.

The noise increased, and eddying gusts of wind swept sharp particles of dust against their ankles.

'I went this far earlier, collecting sticks,' he told her, the light of the torch picking out a litter of dead twigs that the wind had dropped inside. 'Will it be safe to go further?'

They could hear the rain now, a lashing wetness tearing at the vegetation beyond the entrance and melding into the roar of the waves and the ceaseless howling of the wind.

'A little further and we should be able to see how high the tide is,' she told him, but the fury of the storm beyond their shelter was frightening her now, and her feet dragged as she forced them along the increasingly windy passage.

After the darkness of the tunnel, the amount of light surprised her, until she realised it must be close to dawn. Grey seas, white-topped with wind-ripped curds of foam, billowed and roared far closer than she had expected. The rain swept in, almost horizontal to the ground, and the small, stubby bushes that guarded the entrance to the cave whipped this way and that as the elemental fury tried to tear their roots from the earth.

'Makes man seem totally insignificant,' Jack said, staring in awe as nature stirred the sea to a seething tumult, throwing itself again and again against the rocky barrier of the shore. 'If it's high tide or close to high tide now, we should be safe,' he added, the prosaic replacing the poetic. 'The tunnel slopes up away from the sea, and there are no signs that it has encroached far before. No shells or seaweed, the kind of thing you'd expect to see if it happened often.'

Gaby nodded, but her mind was not on the water that might or might not wash into the cave, but on the fearsome beauty of the raging wind and water she saw before her, the turbulent upheaval that seemed to match what was happening in her soul.

I don't care that he's passing through, she decided, because he's married anyway. And if he's not here to stay, it doesn't matter that he's married.

Her mind was as full of foam as the wind that swept in off the ocean, her thoughts as twirled and tumbled as the trees and grass. Yet her body knew, and turned towards the man, who caught it in his arms and held it close.

'A port in the storm, Gaby?' he whispered in her ear.

She shook her head in denial, afraid to speak for fear she'd break the spell that had allowed him to respond to her movement.

She lifted her head and closed her eyes, fearing they might again reveal too much. Lips, salt-flecked, met hers, cold at first, then growing warmer, heating the skin all over her body through the simple contact.

As his tongue slid along the outline of her mouth she opened to him, and felt the invading force slide between her teeth, imparting a hot excitement that thrilled through her body like an electric charge.

A tiny moaning sound limped through the noise that rattled about her ears, and she wondered who had made it. Then his arms tightened, as if in response to that whimper of need, and she felt his body, hard and hot against hers, burning through the shirt, through skin and flesh, and into her bones.

As her knees weakened, he caught her close, then lifted her into his arms and carried her back into the darkness.

He sank to his knees, resting her on the ground in front of him, both kneeling now, arms entangled, hands searching.

'Have you bewitched me, girl?' he asked in the low, rasping voice that made her flesh melt. 'Have you flown me into this furious storm to tear out my heart and send me on my way empty and bereft?' He eased her body away, to arm's length, and one hand stroked her raven hair, trembling on the strands as if the touch might burn him. 'Are you a spirit woman who tempts unwary travellers with visions of splendours mere mortals shouldn't aspire to?'

The words floated past her ears, fanciful, poetic— unbelievable! Inexperience vied with desire, shaking her into a state of such confusion that she wanted to laugh and cry and shout and bellow all at once.

He must be feeling the same attraction she could feel or he wouldn't be speaking this way! And wasn't there a stronger word than attraction? Compulsion was more like it! Was this what sex was all about, this burning, aching, driving, forceful need?

These random wisps of thought flicked in and out of her consciousness, making no sense against the demands of a body that had never felt the force of physical attraction before. Strongest of all the sensations was the desire to feel his arms around her once more, to taste his lips on hers, and find comfort and security against the warmth of his body.

Would he deny her this?

'I am not for you, my Gaby,' he muttered.

Bitterness tainted the words, cooling the air between them; above the storm sounds Gaby heard the wail of the baby and rose to her feet, feeling as if she had aged a hundred years in one long day and night.

She was bending over the fire, dropping more sticks on to it to provide some light, when the howling ceased. The silence was so absolute that Jimmy's whimpers echoed off the walls.

'Is it over?' Lisa whispered the question, afraid to break the unearthly pause.

'I think not,' Gaby told her. 'I think it's the eye passing over us.'

Tension coiled her nerves, making the air they breathed seem brittle, while they all stood and waited.

Was it seconds or hours before they heard the whistling?

'It's crossed the coast,' Gaby said, releasing all her pent-up breath in a loud sigh.

'Is that good or bad?' Jack stood up from his position beside Bernie and walked towards the fire.

'It's good for us because it will lose its ferocity fairly quickly, good for the property owners because it will disintegrate into a low-pressure system and drift across inland, dumping rain where it's needed——'

'And bad?'

She nodded soberly.

'Bad if it's crossed at a settlement. Up here, there are miles and miles of coastline where cyclones can do no harm to anything but the vegetation, but when one chooses to cross at Broome or Derby it could wipe out half a town in a couple of minutes.'

'Although these days new buildings are built to cyclone specifications,' Lisa told him. 'In the old days, the devastation was much worse.'

Jack nodded, his gaze moving from one woman to the other. In the strengthening light, Gaby's eyes caught the flash of blue, and her stomach churned at the knowledge that their time together was all but over.

'And why is our little home whistling now instead of moaning?' Jack asked.

Was the smile that accompanied the question because he was glad the storm was abating? Gaby wondered.

'The wind's blowing from a different direction, that's all,' she explained. 'It swirls around the eye, so before it reaches you you feel the wind that's sweeping downwards from the north or noth-east, and after it's passed you get the other side of the swirl, sweeping upwards from the south.'

'Smart sheila, isn't she?' Lisa said with a smile at Gaby to soften the slang expression.

'More than smart,' Jack replied, a huskiness in his

voice that started Gaby's internal fireworks going again.

As the fire flickered back to life, the dancing light touched his bare torso. She watched the patterns that played across the satiny skin. With a convulsive movement, she reached down and retrieved her uniform.

'I'll change then give you back your shirt,' she said quickly, unable to withstand the distraction of his innocently naked chest.

'I've a spare pair of shorts and a shirt in my bag,' Lisa told her. 'Spare knickers as well.'

She handed Jimmy to Jack, who smiled at the baby and rocked him in his arms while he felt for the baby heartbeats with the fingers of one hand.

'I'll go up to the sheltered end of the tube and have a wash then change,' Gaby said, as the sight of the man with the baby unsettled her even more.

'Be careful, Gaby!' he murmured, stepping towards her as if he would like to stop her.

'I'm not recklessly stupid,' she assured him. 'I know the wind will still be fierce out ther. I'll catch the drips of water from the cave roof for my shower.'

'I could come and hold your clothes,' he offered, and winked at her. As her heart flipped over at the sight of his face, drawn with tiredness yet relaxed into an uncomplicated smile, she wondered how she could ever have thought him hard.

'I'll manage,' she assured him, but wished with all her heart that they were alone in this long cave by the sea, a man and a woman, transported back to the beginnings of time.

'Here you are.' Lisa handed her clean, dry clothes. 'It's a good thing I packed for a few days—we'll both have something to wear. Jack will have to stay

dirty——' she smiled at him '—unless he fancies my
floral dress. It's an old one I had when I was pregnant,
and falls from two ties at the shoulders.'

'He'd look kind of cute in it, I would think,' Gaby
replied as they both fixed their eyes on Jack and
laughed at the image Lisa had conjured up.

'If you take this baby, I'll get breakfast,' he
responded. 'A man could starve to death while you
women worry about clothes.'

The light-hearted banter brought an ease into all
their hearts. Gaby relaxed, knowing the wind would
blow itself out in a few hours, and help would soon be
on the way.

Had anyone heard her messages? she wondered as
she stripped off Jack's shirt and her dirty underwear
and stepped out into the rain. If not, then the search
pattern would follow her original route home—fanning
out from a straight line between Olga Creek and
Derby.

Rubbing herself roughly dry with her soiled uniform,
she dressed, while her mind darted through the
possibilities.

They were west of Olga Creek, but not so far west
that they'd be missed as the search widened. But that
was if the plane was still on the strip, where it would
be easily visible from the air!

She dashed back down the tunnel, stopping when
she could see the reflected light from the fire.

'I'll be a little longer,' she said. 'The wind's not as
bad as it sounds and I need to check the plane.'

She hurried away, not wanting to hear any argu-
ments. It probably wouldn't occur to either of them
that planes could be lifted into the air and carried for a

hundred yards or more, and she wasn't about to worry them by telling them.

Back at the cave entrance, she stripped off the dry clothes, looked distatefully at her wet, grubby uniform and shook her head. It would be cold to put on and the thought of getting back into it made her feel queasy.

'Who's to see me?' she muttered to herself, and, clad only in her rubber-soled shoes, she stepped out into the warm rain, feeling the force of the wind as she emerged into the sheltered hollow. The ferocity of the previous evening was already abating, although it still whipped her sodden hair across her face and the rain still lashed her bare body.

As she jogged up the slight rise so that she could see the tarmac, she took in the damage that had been done. Trees uprooted, branches whipped from trunks, the whole mess strewn about like children's toys after a wild party.

Even from this distance she could see the plane still tilted at an angle towards her. Had the fact that it had slumped towards the fury of the wind saved it? Aeronautically, it was the best way for it to have fallen.

Pleased to see the plane was safe, she turned her attention to the runway. Through the sheeting rain she could make out the litter of debris that would have to be cleared before any rescue plane could land, and she would have to pace out the strip to see how much length there was before anyone coming in was inconvenienced by the Cessna.

Should she she go across and try the radio again?

One more step brought her out into the full force of the wind, and she turned back. It would be safer in another hour, and she would definitely need clothes on to protect her body from the debris that still blew through the air.

She turned and raced back towards their sanctuary. There was so much to do before the weather eased enough to allow planes to take off from other towns.

'Eve in flying boots!'

Jack stood in the cave entrance, the baby still in his arms. His eyes were riveted to her body, and Gaby slowed, then trembled under the intensity of that gaze.

'Lisa insisted on cooking breakfast so I came to check on you,' he said, but the words she heard were different. I love you, he seemed to be saying.

'There's a lot to be done after we've eaten,' she replied, and wondered if he heard the reply beneath her words.

He bent and picked up his shirt which she'd discarded earlier, handing it to her as the came out of the rain.

'Dry yourself on this—it's cleaner than your uniform.' His eyes met hers. 'Please, Gaby,' he whispered, and she knew she had not imagined the silent conversation.

She took the shirt and very slowly slid it down her arms, then pressed her face into its folds and ran it over her hair. With careful concentration, she slid it across her body, aware that he was watching every movement, seeking and learning, but loving, not lustful.

When she was finished she stood before him, presenting herself for his inspection, the first man who had ever seen her naked woman's body.

Wonder, awe, love and agony. Could such a medley of feelings be reflected in one pair of eyes? Gaby glimpsed them all before she moved away, pulling on the dry clothes as if they might shield her from the hurt that she sensed was going to come soon enough.

'I'm trying Jimmy on a little juice,' Jack told her as he walked beside her towards their makeshift camp.

She ran the words over again in her head, but they were simply words, with no secret message ringing within their cadences.

'A blockage of the pyloric sphincter is usually partial, not total. It was only when his stomach was overfull that the projectile vomiting would have occurred. Twenty-four hours without food should have cleared whatever was in there, and a little liquid might keep other complications at bay.'

'We could be out here by midday, the way the weather's clearing,' Gaby told him. 'In case you were saving the milk formula for Bernie.'

He turned to her, and his eyes said that he was sorry, but his lips explained that diluted juice with salts added would be easier for Jimmy to digest.

'Actually, the doctor who sees him will probably test him for allergy to cow's milk and dairy-based formula. An intolerance to dairy products will often result in projectile vomiting in infants.'

'Better than the poor little mite having to have an operation,' Gaby said, then was aware that she'd startled him by the vehemence in her voice.

Of course I want to get away from here, she told herself as she greeted Lisa and began to explain how things were outside. So why is it making me feel so cranky?

'How's Bernie?' she asked, to take her mind off the dissident forces within her.

'He's doing just great,' Jack told her, 'considering all I need to care for him is an ECG machine to monitor his heart, some special formula to replace the trace elements he's losing because of the burn, and some way of testing his urine for sodium and glucose.'

'He's no good, is he?' Gaby demanded, wondering again if she should have flown on instead of stopping.

'His blood-pressure's good—and thank heavens for Carole's bag which at least had a blood-pressure kit. His pulse is higher than I would like but I would expect that considering the trauma of the burns he suffered. The problem is, keeping him pumped full of morphine to ease the pain, I'm getting false readings. The drug slows down blood-pressure, respiratory-rate and heart-rate.'

'Something could be happening underneath that you're not aware of?' Gaby asked.

'Anything could be happening underneath, Gaby,' he answered softly, and again another message slipped through. 'All I'm doing is keeping him comfortable, and you and Lisa could have done that just as well.'

He's tired, that's why he sounds disillusioned and world-weary again, she told herself, before hastening to reassure him.

'Lisa and I wouldn't have had a clue!'

'And we wouldn't have slept a wink all night without a man to protect us,' Lisa told him, stepping forward to take the sleeping baby from his arms. 'Let's eat, then Gaby can tell us what we have to do next. I expect the runway out there is covered with rubbish.'

'You two take all this so calmly,' Jack said as they settled down to a meal of rolled oats and dried fruit. 'Not a trace of hysteria from either of you!'

'Would you have preferred us to go all weak and feeble, to weep and wail and wring our hands in anguish?' Gaby teased, and he shook his head decisively.

'When you live on an isolated property, you tend to learn to fend for yourself. Too often survival depends on common sense, and hysterics might waste the time that could save a life,' Lisa told him.

'You sound experienced,' Jack said, and Gaby took up the story as Lisa shuddered convulsively.

'When Lisa's daughter was just walking, they had extensions done to their house. A gang of carpenters who work the west came through with their huge generators, nail-guns, all the gear——'

'Melissa followed her father over to the new building and was playing in a puddle by the cement mixer,' Lisa explained, taking over and speaking in a hard, dry voice. 'One of their leads must have been frayed—we never really got to the bottom of what happened because they were supposed to have safety cut-out switches on all their gear. . . Anyway, the puddle became electrified and her heart stopped beating.'

Gaby picked up the story.

'Mark brought her into the house and they began CPR. She came round almost immediately, but if either of them had waited to have a good cry first there could have been irreversible damage.'

'And did you contact the Flying Doctor immediately that time or wait for the next clinic flight?' Jack asked, and under the teasing lilt of the words they could hear wonder and admiration vying for control of his voice.

'Once we were certain she was breathing OK on her own. We were so frightened by what had happened, we both stood and shook for a while, then rang the doctor.'

'And that makes it hard for the service,' Gaby added.

'Because flights are expensive, someone has to decide what flights are necessary.'

'And how does the omnipotent person decide that?' He looked into her eyes as he asked the question, sending tremors she couldn't control coursing through her once again.

'It's a kind of scale. Life-dependent, life-threatening, deterioration in a patient's condition if help isn't obtained. Melissa's fingers were badly burnt. Delay in getting her to medical care could have resulted in permanent damage.'

'Plus the fact that her parents might both have passed out with shock if left to cope on their own for any length of time,' Lisa added. 'I really didn't believe she was still alive until the doctor arrived and told me so!'

Jack chuckled.

'With two such formidably efficient females for company, I could probably survive out here forever, but people will be worrying about us, I guess, so we'd better begin to get organised.'

He turned to Gaby.

'What's the first job? You be the boss and I'll be the muscle.'

Her gaze swept involuntarily up his arms, taking in the strong biceps, the rounded strength of his shoulders and the flat slabs of muscle on his chest. 'People will be worrying', he'd said, but the only 'people' who would know he was missing was the ice-cool blonde called Lauren.

And he hadn't once mentioned her, not yesterday when they had been together all day, nor during the night, when he had—and hadn't quite—flirted with her.

CHAPTER SIX

THEY delegated Lisa to watch over Bernie, Jack handing her a whistle from the emergency pack to hang around her neck in case she needed to summon help.

'If you come to the mouth of the cave and blow that, we should be able to hear you,' he told her. Gaby opened her mouth to argue but he hurried her away.

'It will make her feel less cut off from us,' he whispered, walking close beside her so that he could hiss the words into her ear. 'I'll go back and check that all is well in a couple of hours anyway.'

Gaby nodded, pleased that he had considered how Lisa might feel when they both left the cave. He's caring in a thoughtful way, she realised, not solely a medical way.

'We've got to clear debris from the strip and make sure our plane can be clearly seen from the air,' she told him as they came to the cave entrance. 'When the weather clears enough for a search to be organised, they will look for the plane.'

'Or wreckage, I suppose,' he added, and she shuddered, crossing her fingers as she hoped, yet again, that her desperate messages had reached someone.

They paused at the mouth of the wide tunnel, watching the rain that fell so relentlessly.

'I understand now why you Australians call this time of the year the wet,' Jack said. 'That sure describes it! Perhaps we'll forget about trying to keep dry.' He dropped the tarpaulin he was carrying on to the ground. 'If the wind is still flinging big missiles about, then it's too dangerous for us to be starting clean-up operations.'

Gaby turned to face him, acknowledging the common-sense decision. He had put on his damp blue shirt, and the wet material clung to his torso, delineating the shape, while the colour accentuated the blueness of his eyes. Her heart teetered for a moment, then flipped over again.

'You've got to watch for snakes, although they should still be in shelter while the rain persists, and keep your back to the wind as much as possible, to protect your eyes and face from flying rubbish.' The words tripped over each other as her clumsy tongue pretended that nothing unusual was happening between them. And was it between them, or was she the only one affected?

'Your eyes go black as charcoal when you're being bossy.'

Her mouth opened, then closed again. She drew a deep breath, held it for a moment, then let it out in a long sigh. She wasn't the only one! She couldn't be!

'We've got work to do,' she whispered, as soon as she could find enough co-ordination to speak. 'Firstly, I want to go back to the plane and send out another message. Then, as soon as we've cleared a bit of the runway, I want to use branches to spell out "All OK" as close to the plane as possible.'

He spun towards her, his abrupt movement challenging the statement.

'You're not certain your messages have got through?'

Did he sound upset? Was he concerned for his wife? For the woman he'd called Lauren?

She shrugged uneasily.

'Without confirmation it's impossible to tell. I've sent the messages in the hope that someone might pick them up and pass them on to the relevant authorities, but whatever is wrong with the radio could be preventing it sending as well as receiving. If you don't get a response, you can't be certain of anything.'

'You didn't tell Lisa that!' It was a neutral observation.

'So she could have something more to concern her? So she could spend the night lying awake worrying about Mark worrying about her and Jimmy?'

And you could worry about your wife worrying? she added silently.

He nodded his understanding.

'We'll stay together and work together. Plane first,' was all he said, then he took her hand and they walked out into the streaming wetness.

The little plane might still have been where she had left it, but it was inaccessible. Uprooted trees and bushes and miscellaneous scraps of junk that shouldn't have been this far from civilisation had been flung against it. They worked steadily, pulling the rubbish away bit by bit, sharing the weight of the larger pieces, dragging and pushing, until they had cleared a small area of tarmac around the plane and she had access to the door.

While Jack continued to drag rubbish to one side of the strip, Gaby sent out her message, repeating it again and again as she had the previous evening, until her voice cracked with the strain.

'I've cleared a space and spelt out the message on the narrower strip of the runway on the far side of the plane,' he told her as she emerged from the comparative shelter of the wing.

'With this weather, a plane would have to land into the wind,' she told him, the wind catching her voice and tossing it past him, 'so we'll clear this end of the runway first.'

She waved her hand to indicate the direction, her eyes making a visual assessment of the situation, measuring the width of the strip and adjacent clearing beside the immobilised plane. A plane landing into the wind would be bogged within seconds if it left the hard strip. Would there be enough runway between here and the end?

I won't know until I pace it out. She answered her own question, saying the words in her head as she did in all her pre-flight preambles. It has to be this end, she concluded, because at the moment a light aircraft couldn't land from the other direction.

She bent her back and began to drag twisted debris off the runway, pulling it towards the eastern side of the strip. Jack bent with her and although they worked in silence, conserving all their energy for the task, she was aware of his presence, and felt an easy companionship that added an extra impetus to her endeavours.

'How far do you think it is from here back to the plane?' she asked as they finally both slumped to the ground in the lee of one of their rubbish piles.

He turned towards her and she saw the flash of concern in his eyes, then his hand reached out and lifted wet strands of hair from her face.

Was she as dirty and dedraggled-looking as he was? she wondered. She tried a wobbly smile in a valiant effort to appear less exhausted.

'Oh, Gaby!' he sighed, his fingers fluttering against her wet skin, pushing at the water that slid down from her hair.

Rain and wind lashed around them, but the small space they occupied became a cocoon of silence as unspoken messages passed between them.

Gaby lifted one hand and pressed his against her cheek, marvelling at its warmth despite the deluge that had soaked them both to the skin.

'I have to know how far it is,' she said at last, struggling to her feet when the yearning in her body to lean against him became too strong for her to combat any longer. 'I have to send another message and that information will be vital.'

He rose to stand beside her, looking down at her with incomprehension.

'You stay here and rest—I'll step it out,' he ordered with a frown that made her want to weep.

'I'll come. I have to try the radio.'

The words were lost in the wind, and she struggled after him, but he had moved away so swiftly that she couldn't catch up. A sense of loss settled heavily about her as his finger became indistinct, blurred to an insubstantial shadow by the rain.

Of course she must do everything in her power to be rescued! She wanted to be rescued, she reminded herself, battling into the wind. Yet part of her denied it, knowing that something which hadn't even begun would end with the arrival of help.

Tears—of tiredness, she decided stoutly—mingled with the rain as she plodded back towards the plane.

She heard the clacking beat of the helicopter long before she saw it, and gazed up in astonishment as the huge, ungainly craft became recognisable. Khaki, green and grey, its camouflage worked as well in cyclonic weather as it would over a jungle.

Jack ran from beside the plane and scooped her up

in his arms, racing back into its lee and bending over
her as the rotors whipped rain and small bits of debris
into a man-made storm.

'Gaby Forsythe?'

The tall man in army fatigues dropped out and came
towards them, bent low, and yelling the words above
the noise of the slowing blades.

Gaby nodded, but nestled closer into Jack's still
sheltering arms. So little time together. It should have
been forever—her heart knew that—but fate had
decreed otherwise, and she would lose him.

'I'm Brian Ward. You all Ok?' the man asked as he
came closer. Jack straightened up and held out his
hand in greeting. He introduced himself with the
formal courtesy that seemed so much a part of him,
then went on to explain.

'We've got a patient with severe burns and a heart
problem in a cave Miss Forsythe found.' He nodded
towards the shelter. 'And an infant we were bringing
into town for possible surgery. Do you have a
stretcher—and some oilskins, or something to cover
the mother and child when we bring them across to the
chopper?'

He had taken over, Gaby realised, slumping back on
to the ground.

'We've stretchers, and oilskins, but how about we
get this lady out of the rain first?' the stranger suggested, walking across to where Gaby sat shivering.
'Looks like she's on her last legs.'

'It's reaction,' Jack told him, forestalling the new-
comer's move to bend and help Gaby to her feet. 'And
exhaustion, I would say. It's thanks to her we're all still
alive.'

He smiled into her eyes as he lifted her, but she didn't want his gratitude and turned her head away.

'Your father said you'd be here.' Brian fell in beside Jack as he carried her towards the men who were jumping from the belly of the big craft. 'He's been in touch with every authority on this side of Australia. He insisted something must have happened and, as you couldn't go back to some place called Olga Creek in the bad weather, you'd have headed for here.'

'They didn't get the messages?' Gaby asked, drawn out of her private misery by the man's strange statement.

'Not a word,' he told her, leading Jack towards the door of the helicopter. 'Mind you, the cyclone swung south-east and crossed the coast about twenty kilometres north of Derby. It was a Category Four blow and has caused some structural damage in the town. Radio masts would have been the first things to go.'

'Someone, somewhere would have heard it if that damn radio had been working,' she muttered. It was good to release some of her tension in anger, especially as it could be directed at an inanimate object and do no harm!

'It's OK now—they've found us,' Jack whispered soothingly, pressing her a fraction closer against his chest.

He doesn't know that's why I'm cross, she thought sadly, and wriggled in his arms, wanting to be free of such gross insensitivity!

'Where have you guys dropped from?' he asked as he eased her down into the open door.

'We were on a training exercise between Wyndham and Darwin. We flew into Wyndham before the cyclone turned south, intending to hold position there ready for rescue missions.'

A warm blanket was wrapped around Gaby's shoulders.

'Take care of her,' Jack said to the two men still in the aircraft. 'A hot cup of tea with plenty of sugar would help if you can rustle one up.'

Then he was gone, leading the group of young soldiers towards their temporary shelter.

Gaby watched him walk away, noticing that the tension was gone from his step. He might be tired, but he had also unwound, somehow. Were his fainting spells caused by the strain she had sensed in him earlier? Would this unwinding mean the end of them?

Someone pressed a hot cup of tea into her hands, suggesting that she might like to move into one of the seats. She shook her head, watching the little group grow smaller then finally disappear into the depression that marked the entrance to their cave.

'We'll take you back to Wyndham. There's a doctor standing by for your patients,' one of the servicemen told her. 'We're leaving Derby free for the State Emergency Service teams and the service personnel flying in to organise and carry out the mopping-up operations.'

'You've sent word out that we're all safe?' Gaby asked, realising that four sets of family and friends would have spent an extremely anxious night.

'Soon as we sighted your message,' the man assured her. 'If you're Miss Forsythe, I reckon your dad will be at Wyndham as soon as flying conditions clear enough for his small plane. It was only when we said we'd definitely come down here to look for you that he agreed to stay at home until the weather cleared.'

The thought of her father's determination made her smile, but it was a wan effort while her heart lay so heavily in her chest.

Figures appeared on the horizon, and the little procession made its way towards the plane. Two soldiers carried Bernie on a stretcher between them, the next man carried Jimmy, a tarp providing shelter for both bodies, while a fourth held a raincoat over Lisa's head and helped her across the rough terrain. Behind them were Jack and the man in charge, laden down with the bags, swags and emergency gear from the plane.

As they came closer, she saw the efficiency of these trained men. Two lifted Bernie into the plane and slotted the stretcher into position along one wall. The drip bottle was hung on a hook above him, warm blankets produced and wrapped around him, while another man seemed to be taking his blood-pressure.

'We carry a medical orderly,' Bernie explained, seeing her interest in the competent way the patient was handled. 'In peacetime we do a lot of rescue work. It's good practice for us, and more practical than the usual over-imaginative exercises our bosses dream up for us.'

She nodded and almost smiled, telling herself it was time to relax and let these men take over all her problems.

'Do you want anything out of the plane?' Brian asked.

She glanced towards the little Cessna and saw two men bent over the crippled wheel strut. They straighted as another man drew closer, and she heard voices raised as they yelled through the rain.

'I don't think so,' she replied, watching the men coming towards the helicopter to report to their leader.

'No damage to the wing and only minor repairs needed to straighten out the wheel,' one announced. 'It shouldn't take much effort to patch her up enough for someone to fly her out.'

Gaby tried another smile. If she practised enough, she might get better at it, she decided, realising the spontaneous grin which used to spring to life so frequently was probably gone forever. Lisa was helped into the helicopter now, and Jimmy handed up to her.

The baby was too quiet and listless to be well, Gaby acknowledged, and again she was forced to question the decision she had made.

'The rest of the runway needs clearing if a bigger plane is to land here,' she said, hoping that practical matters might blot out her despair.

'We'll leave a couple of fellows to do that, and our engineer will stay and tinker with that wheel. He'll have a radio and will let us know what needs to be brought in before we leave Wyndham this afternoon.'

Brian spoke again to his men, then ushered Jack up into the helicopter, speaking to him in an undertone too low for Gaby to hear as they passed by her.

They'd get to Wyndham and be back by this afternoon? Gaby thought. It was all happening too quickly! This helicopter would drop them in Wyndham and be back here *this afternoon*! And Jack? The cyclone was little inducement for him to stay on at this edge of the English-speaking world through the wet. By this time tomorrow he could be well on his way—back to the other world where he belonged.

But he belongs to me! her heart whispered, as an

undercurrent of noise from the low-accented voice drifted into her ears.

'. . .no sign of recent occupation,' he was saying, and she frowned, wondering what the exclusive male conversation was about.

'. . .drugs!' the other man said, and she shivered. Had the Army been in the area for less innocent reasons than an exercise?

She stood up carefully, moving to a seat by the outer wall of the helicopter and automatically fastening her seatbelt. Jack was up towards the front and all she could see was the back of his dark, wet head.

'. . .exciting!' Lisa had twisted in her seat to speak to her but she was unable to concentrate on anything. With a fierce determination, she focused on Jack's back. If he turns around and looks at me, even just glances over his shoulder to check that I'm all right, I'll be happy, she promised herself.

But he didn't move, and it didn't matter anyway, she decided, because deep down she knew it wasn't true. Knew she might never again be truly happy—in the simple, uncomplicated way she had always accepted as her right.

She tipped back her head against the metal skin of the machine and closed her eyes, hoping to keep back the stupid tears welling up from her aching soul.

Something fell to the ground with a clatter and people moved around her, leaning over her, speaking to her, but she slipped away from them all, into a world where Jack's arms still held her and his breath brushed softly against her cheek.

'Wake up, sleepyhead!'

Was that Lisa's voice?

Her eyelids shot open and her body tensed for

action, then she realised they were no longer in the cave.

With detached bewilderment, she watched as the men in army uniform released Bernie's stretcher and lifted him, stretcher and all, out of the helicopter. She could remember seeing him strapped in, and tried to piece together other fragments of memory.

'We're in Wyndham,' Lisa explained, rocking Jimmy in her arms. 'You were asleep before we took off!'

Gaby shook her head, recalling the fuzzy events of the morning. And Jack? She looked quickly towards the front of the cabin, but the dark head was gone.

He would need to go with Bernie, she told herself. To tell the doctor who was taking over what he had been given, and when.

'You OK?' she asked Lisa. 'And Jimmy?'

'We're going to the hospital with Bernie,' she responded. 'I'm sorry to go off like this, but the sooner I can get him treated, the sooner I can get back to Mark. If we've had all this rain at home, he'll be needing an extra hand.'

'Of course you've got to go,' Gaby told her. 'If I'd flown on yesterday——and was it only yesterday? her tired mind asked '—you would already have seen the doctor and would be on your way to having the problem sorted out.'

'Or we could have been blown away when the cyclone struck,' Lisa told her with a mischievous grin. 'We were probably far safer in our nice solid cave than in Derby, from all accounts. What are you going to do?'

'Find a shop and buy some clean clothes. I seem to have made rather a mess of your shirt and shorts.' She looked down at the torn, filthy remnants of Lisa's clothes with an apologetic grimace. 'Then I'll have the longest, hottest shower I have ever had. After that, I might be able to think!'

'You deserve to have whatever you wish for,' Lisa murmured, as one of their rescuers came back to help her and Jimmy out of the helicopter. 'You looked after us all so well.'

She passed the baby down to the waiting arms, then gave Gaby a quick hug, before following the man out into the greyness of the rain.

Me next, Gaby thought, but she lacked the will to move. The man she'd met first climbed in and came to squat beside her. His name was Brian, she remembered, and he seemed to be the boss. What rank would the boss be? she wondered vaguely, her mind wandering off at a tangent again.

'The ambulance is leaving now with all your passengers. It's full up but we could arrange other transport to the hospital for you so they can check you out.'

'No, I'm OK,' she told him. 'A little tired maybe, but nothing that a bath and sleep won't cure.'

'I'll get someone to run you into town, then,' he suggested, sounding so kind and helpful that she wanted to cry again.

She looked at him, noticing him as an individual for the first time. His soft, golden-brown eyes were looking at her with admiration. Admiration that was for her as a person, not for her face or her figure. For some reason he made her feel safe and secure.

'I'd like a lift to town,' she said, and smiled.

He smiled back, and his face shone with simple, good-natured delight. 'I'll fix it,' he promised, standing up but still hovering close.

'What about the gear from the plane?' She remem-

bered she had other responsibilities besides her passengers. 'I'm not concerned about the food, but the
emergency pack and the swags. I should keep an eye
on them and at least take that much back with me to
Derby.'

'Worried the boss will yell at you for denting his
plane?' he teased.

'It wasn't even one of our own planes,' she told him
gloomily. 'It was chartered to do the clinic flight and a
doctor's visit to Kalumburu next week. I was the one
who insisted that the little Cessna with the door modi-
fication was all we needed. The boss wanted to get
something bigger but we'd have had to hire it in Perth
and fly it up, and it seemed so much fuss when the
four-seater available in Broome would do the job.'

'Think what a mess you'd have made of the bigger
plane when you hit that drum. And the cost of lifting
the wreck out of that place! At least the Cessna will be
able to be patched up and flown out.'

She smiled at him again.

'You're only saying that to make me feel better,' she
said.

'Did it work?' he asked, and his eyes grew serious
for a moment—as if he really cared how she felt!

'Not as well as a hot shower will,' she told him light-
heartedly. 'You will take care of the gear for me? If it's
left at the terminal building here, and marked RFDS,
I can collect it and take it with me when I fly back to
Derby.'

'I'll guard it with my life, Miss Forsythe,' he promised, with a snappy salute that made her chuckle. 'I
could keep saluting, if it kept you laughing,' he said,
reaching down a hand to help her out of her seat.

He's flirting with me, she realised, and the thought,

which yesterday would have aggravated her, today made her feel warm and safe. If she hadn't been so tired, would his gentle banter have affected her differently?

She walked stiffly behind him to the door and dropped down on to the tarmac.

'Umbrella, miss!' One of the men held a wide airport umbrella over her head and she hovered beneath its protection, uncertain where to go or what to do next.

'The car will be here in a moment,' Brian told her, ducking his head into the shelter of the umbrella. 'We've booked you into the Wyndham Town hotel— and told them to look after you there.'

She thanked him as a car drew up beside them. One of the younger army men was driving, and Brian opened the door and ushered her in.

'Do you need money? Someone to do some shopping for you?'

Gaby looked around the young men standing by the helicopter watching her depature.

'Which of them would you send into a lingerie shop?' she asked, grinning at the group.

'You find a lingerie shop in Wyndham and I'll personally go in and choose something—ah, suitable!— for you,' he responded quickly.

'I think I'll manage!' she assured him, and dropped into the back seat of the car.

She was whisked away, arriving within minutes at the hotel. The proprietor was a stranger, but she greeted Gaby as if she'd known her all her life.

'Your dad's been on the phone,' the woman told her. 'Rang the shop, and they've sent up a few bags of clothes for you. I've put them in your room. There are tea things and biscuits in there as well,' she added, leading Gaby towards the motel units. 'But if you'd like something more substantial to eat, I'll get it for you. Dinner in the dining-room from six, and, though I say it myself, they're the best meals in town. And don't worry about money—your dad said he'd fix it all up.'

Reaching their destination, she unlocked a door and pushed it open. The air-conditioner hummed quietly, and the chill made Gaby shiver in her damp clothes.

'I'll turn that off for a while,' the woman said, noticing the involuntary movement. 'You can turn it back on when you're clean and dry.'

Gaby thanked the kind, motherly soul, but then ushered her out of the door and shut it firmly before she fussed any more. Her own beautiful, vague, talented mother never fussed—although her father did enough for both of them, she admitted silently.

The promised clothes were in five large paper carrier bags on the huge bed. She walked across and tipped them out, smiling at the array of underwear, shorts and shirts, casual dresses, night attire and toiletries her father considerd necessary for a night or two in Wyndham.,

Selecting soap, toothpaste—now why didn't the emergency pack contain that necessity?—hair shampoo and conditioner, she headed for the bathroom.

The mirror showed a dirty, bedraggled urchin, with dark eyes huge in her pale, strained face. The wet clothes clung to her body, blood colouring them pinky where sharp spikes had torn through the cloth and into her skin. Black streaks decorated her forehead and chin, and a scratch that was already showing an angry redness at its edges marked her neck from ear to collarbone.

She peeled off the sodden garments and dropped them all into the rubbish bin. She'd buy new shorts and a shirt for Lisa one day, she promised herself, turning slowly in front of the mirror to see if there was more unseen damage.

Her body looked the same as it had always looked, but she knew it had changed. Some strange chemical had been released, and the long quiescent time was over.

She turned on the shower as hard as it would go and stepped under it—cold water at first, then gradually warming it—hoping she could clean away the strange new craving with the dirt.

Half an hour later she was clean. Her hair was dry for the first time in twenty-four hours, thanks to someone's forethought in leaving a drier in the bathroom, and she was wearing new dry clothes—attractive white linen shorts and a sleeveless linen top, with heavy white-on-white embroidery following the low, rounded neckline.

Had her father dictated her clothes preference—or his? she wondered, but she smiled at her reflection, then wished that Jack were there.

She made a cup of tea and carried it over to the bed, intending to lie down and read the information about Wyndham in the folder on the bedside table. Then she'd think a little about all that had happened so that she could sort it out in her mind.

She'd think about the scheduled flight, about the unexpected things that had cropped up during the day, about the patients she'd collected, and maybe, when she'd though about all of that, she'd think, just a little, about Jack!

CHAPTER SEVEN

WAS it the increasing mugginess of the room or the door opening that woke her? Gaby forced her sticky eyelids apart, and saw the dark figure in the doorway.

'I was worried about you! Mrs Grant said she hadn't seen or heard from you since she showed you into the room four hours ago.'

The husky whisper trailed like a feather across her skin, while her sleep-fogged mind registered his anxiety with pleasure.

'Gaby?'

No one would ever say 'Gaby' in quite that way again! The thought made her want to cry, so she smiled at him to hide the weakness, and shuffled her limbs together until she was in a sitting position on the bed.

'It's hot in here. The air-conditioning's off!' she said. Strange words to hear issuing from her mouth when what she wanted to say was, Come in, Jack. Hold me!

He moved into the room, but only as far as the control switch, turning on the unit with a sharp click that echoed in the uneasy silence. The door swung shut, leaving the room shadowed.

'Mrs Grant let me in, but only after I'd told her I was a doctor and I needed to check on you.' There was a pause, then he repeated the last words with an incomprehensible emphasis. 'I did need to check on you!'

The air-conditioning unit creaked and whirred as it stirred itself to battle the moisture-laden humidity.

What can I say to him? Gaby wondered as her mind pushed unacceptable words almost on to her tongue.

'I waited while they did an ECG on Bernie,' he said, propping himself against the bench that ran along one wall of the room. 'It was the sudden onset of dyspnea, that irregular, laboured kind of breathing, that suggested a heart problem of some kind, but the morphine Carole had given him had knocked him out, so I couldn't find out if he any chronic heart disease, or even a respiratory problem.'

'Like asthma?' she asked, knowing there was no way she could say what was in her heart.

'Yes!' he agreed. 'But whether it was his heart or respiratory distress of some other kind he needed oxygen and he needed it urgently.'

'You're saying I did the right thing landing when I did?'

Had he realised how worried she had been about that decision? Was he explaining all of this to ease her mind?

He nodded gravely.

'You could have saved the man's life by landing when you did,' he told her. 'The ECG has shown one site of heart muscle injury—slight, but defintely there. By stabilising him as quickly as we did we may have prevented the more serious incident that often follows soon after the initial onset of pain.'

'I risked all your lives by landing where I did,' she muttered, still bothered by the nagging remnants of her earlier guilt

'Nonsense,' he told her. 'You did everything you could have done to get us safely down. If that drum hand't been on the runway, we could have taken off ten or fifteen minutes after landing, as soon as I had an oxygen mask in place.'

The words were reassuring, but when they failed to soothe her inner agitation she realised that it wasn't her actions that were causing her such inner turmoil, but this man's transient presence in her life.

'We were probably better off where we were,' he continued, as if sensing she was still uneasy. 'There's been one man killed and other people injured in Derby.'

'I should be back there,' she said fretfully. 'They'll need pilots to fly injured people out.'

'Pilots are no good without planes,' he told her. 'The airport was in the direct path of Elvie.'

'But when it changed direction and swung towards Derby, planes that aren't hangered would have been flown out—south to Broome, or east to strips on properties.'

'And whoever flew them out will fly them back in when the debris is cleared, and be there to fly injured people out if necessary, without you having to rushing back like a knight to the rescue.'

He smiled at her, but it was more like a grimace than a smile.

'And Jimmy?'

She wanted to keep him talking, wanted him to stay where she could see and hear him, even if it wouldn't be for long!

'He's doing well, the little tyke. They've put him on a more sustaining drip than we could manage, and will test him for allergies before doing any investigative surgery for pyloric stenosis.' He paused, smiling again. 'I wonder what would faze that Lisa?' he mused, shaking his head as if still amazed at her good-natured acceptance of everything that had come their way.

'Nothing much, I imagine,' Gaby told him, smiling herself now.

Then he yawned, his body expanding then relaxing— slumping back against the bench.

'You should be sleeping,' she said, contrarily concerned now, and angry with herself for keeping him standing there when he was obviously exhausted.

'I will be, as soon as someone finds me a spare bed,' he said, and this time the smile was more genuine, softening the gauntness of his face.

'There are no rooms?' she demanded, leaping off the bed and walking towards him.

'With all roads to the south blocked by this deluge you people call rain? The town's jam-packed. From all accounts, your father ordered the Army to remove a family of ten from this room so you could have a bed.'

He chuckled when he saw her straighten, and held up his hand in surrender.

'No, that's not true,' he assured her, 'although, from what Brian Ward and Mrs Grant have told me, he would have done if nothing had been available.'

Now she could see the colour in his eyes, the blueness that fascinated and tantalised her. He was so close, she could have reached out and touched him, but he was not hers to touch.

'Sleep here,' she said hoarsely. There's a bathroom through there, with plenty of good thick towels.'

She rummaged through the gear that still lay strewn on one side of the bed, gathering up the clothes and carrying them across to the small wardrobe.

'Here's a towelling gown that will keep you more or

less decent. I'll go out and get you some fresh clothes while you're sleeping.'

'Don't be kind to me, Gaby,' he said, his voice so strained that she forgot he wasn't hers. She crossed the space between them and drew him into her arms.

'You were kind to me first,' she whispered, holding his hard, muscle-packed body tightly against hers. She kissed his cheek, then stepped away, pausing only to run the new brush through her hair and pull her shirt straight before picking up the room keys and stepping out into the unrelenting rain.

She borrowed a raincoat from Mrs Grant, then walked down the road to use a public phone. Sue Reynolds, a friend from school who was now nursing at Wyndham Hospital, greeted her with gibes about crash-landings.

'You'd think someone who's been flying since she was twelve would have learnt to check the runway was clear before she landed,' she teased.

'I was more worried about the wretched donkeys than old fuel drums left on the surface,' Gaby confessed, cheered by the warm respect underlying Sue's flippancy.

'Do you want a bed for the night?' Sue asked. 'I believe the town's full up.'

'N-o-o-o!' The word slid hesitantly out. Jack had not slept at all the previous night, nor had he caught up during the day, as she had. Once he fell asleep, there was little chance of him waking before morning, so she could sleep on the side of the big bed. She rationalised the decision quickly in her mind. 'What I would like is a book on epilepsy, if you happen to still have your old textbooks with you.'

'Is your mum worse?'

'No, she's fine,' Gaby assured her concerned friend. 'It's just that I know so little about it, and I thought it was time I learned.'

'There's only a small percentage of hereditary factors in it, Gaby.' Now it was Sue providing the reassurance, guessing the wrong reason for Gaby's interest. 'And usually they are associated with a genetic disorder in which epilepsy is a symptom.'

'I know that much, silly!' Gaby told her. 'I'm not worried about myself; Mum was struck on the head by the boom on a sailing boat when she was in her teens. She sustained a three-corner fracture of the skull and was in a coma for some weeks.' She repeated the old story easily.

'I didn't know that,' Sue said. 'I always assumed it must have been some brain damage at birth. So she wasn't always epileptic?'

'Not till she was pregnant with me,' Gaby explained. 'The doctors think there must have been some undetected brain damage that only manifested itself with the hormonal changes of pregnancy. She was told not to have another child, and Sam was an accident. She didn't tell Dad until it was too late to do anything about it, and went ahead with the pregnancy. Her seizures did become more frequent, but really she's so well-balanced on her medication that few people are aware she has a problem.'

'So if you know all this, why the books?'

It was an obvious question for Sue to ask, and Gaby hesitated.

'I know about Mum's case,' but would like to know enough to understand why and how it happens,' she said, hoping Sue would accept the reply without more questions. 'And I'm going to be stuck in Wyndham in the pouring rain for at least twenty-four hours! What else is there for me to do?'

'Fair enough! I'm on night duty at the moment, which is why you caught me at home. Are you staying at the Town?' Barely waiting for Gaby's reply, she continued, 'I'll drop in whatever I've got on my work to work and phone you tomorrow when I've had some sleep. If you're still in town, we could meet for lunch.'

That's one thing done, Gaby decided as she eased out of the phone booth and headed for K's Fashions—Wyndham's clothes emporium. Once there, she realised she would have to guess Jack's size.

'Well, who might this clean young lady be?'

She spun around. Brian Ward and four other young soldiers were gathered in the doorway of the shop.

'You're the very man I need,' Gaby said to him, welcoming his presence with a wide smile. 'Jack finished at the hospital and came across to the hotel for a sleep. I said I'd get him some clean, dry clothes and know nothing about men's sizes.'

What a stupid thing to say! she thought crossly as she felt a tide of colour wash across her cheeks.

Brian's twitching smile made matters worse.

'Now, how big would you say that Yank was?' he drawled, and the other men chuckled as he held out his arms in a parody of an embrace.

'That's what I'm asking you, stupid,' Gaby said, more flustered than she should have been. 'The man was a total stranger, wished on me by the boss yesterday morning. He's shorter than you, and sort of broader somehow.' She stumbled over the words, then looked at the men. 'About that fellow's size, wouldn't you say?'

She appealed to Brian, but her eyes asked more than

that question. Don't tease me, help me, they begged, and she saw the mocking smile fade, and a look of admiration cross his face.

You shouldn't flirt with Brian, an inner voice warned, but thoughts of Jack consumed her mind, and her determination to take care of him for the little time they would still have together overrode all other considerations.

'What size are you, Rosco?' Brian asked, leading the most likely of the candidates forward and looking critically at him as he twirled around. 'Whatever it is, you'll do. Go with Miss Forsythe and try on what she chooses. We might as well do the right thing by the fellow. He's bound to be a local hero and will need to look spiffy for the television cameras.'

The other men laughed. There was little national interest or press coverage of events that happened this far away from Australia's main centres of civilisation.

The man called Rosco followed Gaby into the shop, while the others drifted away.

'Jeans do him?' he asked as she stopped at the menswear section.

'No, moleskins, I reckon,' she said, grinning at the man. Jack could buy the same jeans in America, but she doubted he'd get genuine moleskin trousers over there. At least he'd have something in his wardrobe for the next few years to remind him of Australia. 'And a blue cotton shirt with two pockets. You can do the underwear and socks.'

She paused, walking through the menswear stock, touching this and that.

'And a nightshirt, don't you think?' she asked, pulling out a dark blue satin creation with cartoon characters dancing all over it. 'Marvin the Martian, isn't it?'

They were both laughing now.

'And boxer shorts to match,' Rosco said, gathering up more merchandise into his arms. 'And here's a matching robe! Too much?' He held out his load, but Gaby shook her head.

'Just try the trousers and shirt. Go for bigger rather than smaller; the man has muscles.'

'And so do I,' Rosco told her with mock-reproach, depositing the goods on to a counter and disappearing behind a curtain to try on the clothes that needed to fit.

'How's it going?'

Brian had returned, a plastic carrier bag dangling from his fingers.

'Fine, I think! What have you been buying?'

He handed her the bag.

'I thought the Army could kick in with toiletries for the bloke,' he said. 'Him being a foreigner and all.'

Gaby peered inside then lifted her head and smiled at him.

'That's so kind. I'd never have known what he needed.'

'Pay me back by having dinner with me tonight at the pub?' he asked, the easy smile flickering in his eyes.

'I. . .I really. . .!' She stopped, unable to put all the ifs and buts and maybes into words. 'I'll definitely be eating there,' she said, starting with the one thing that was certain. 'And I'd love to have your company!' That was another truth. At least when she was with people the nagging unhappiness could be held at bay. 'But we may be a threesome,' she explained. 'Jack may wake up, and I can hardly leave him sitting on his own in the same dining-room.'

'I could cope with that—for tonight!' Brian said. 'Jack and I can fight a duel after dinner for the honour of escorting you home. Didgeridoos at twenty paces!'

She had to laugh again. His silly, easy humour was exactly what she needed to banish her despondency.

'As I'm staying at the pub, it's only about twenty paces home!'

Rosco reappeared, announcing that the clothes would be perfect for the absent American. Gaby thanked both men and said goodbye, then gathered up the assortment they had selected. She should reject the cartoon nightshirt and the boxer shorts, she told herself, but she remembered Jack's tired, strained face and decided he needed a bit of frivolity in his life.

She arranged with the storekeeper to add the new clothes to her father's account, and left with an assortment of brown paper bags.

Jack was lying beneath the sheet, deeply asleep, when she returned to her room. Slipping the packages to the ground, she stood and watched him, a strange guilt creeping over her, as if she was stealing this time, and this sight.

With a desperation born of that guilt, she studied his features, trying to analyse what it was in a straight, thin nose, wide but not full lips, dark eyelashes on tanned skin that could possibly have attracted her so unexpectedly.

I must print the image in my mind, she thought, noticing again the tiny white scar that made one eyebrow quirk upwards.

His shoulders lifted as he breathed deeply, and her eyes were drawn to the bare skin showing above the sheet. It was pale and silky smooth—tight over the flat planes of muscle that moulded its shape.

This is voyeurism, her mind protected, but still she feasted on the sight of him, devouring the contours of his body, the shadow in the angle of neck and chin, the long fingers on the hand that rested on the pillow. She closed her eyes, imagining the feel of those fingers on her bare skin——

A light tap on the door brought her back to her senses.

'I was watching for you to come back,' Mrs Grant whispered through the crack that Gaby had opened. 'Your dad rang while you were out. Said he would be here tomorrow to collect you, weather permitting.'

'Thanks, Mrs Grant. And thanks for the raincoat.' She shrugged out of the damp garment and handed it back. 'I'll come down to the office shortly and phone Dad.' That should have been the first thing she did, she realised guiltily. This man was disrupting her life to the point of madness! 'Dr Fletcher's asleep in here at the moment. He was up all night last night, and I had a good sleep this afternoon while he was still at the hospital.'

As Mrs Grant gave a knowing nod and walked away, Gaby realised that she sounded as if she was making excuses for having a man in her room. If he'd been there for any reason other than lack of space elsewhere, she would have been the happiest woman on earth, and no excuses would have been considered.

She dismissed the stupid sadness that the thought provoked and followed Mrs Grant towards the office.

'There's a package here for you as well,' the proprietor announced when Gaby walked in. 'I forgot to take it up earlier. Sue Reynolds dropped it in.'

Gaby thanked her, then phoned home, speaking to her mother and reassuring her that all was well.

'I knew that, pet,' her mother said calmly. 'I kept telling your father, but he does fuss so! Now, make the most of the present. There's a bit of rough weather ahead, but you'll come through in the end. Goodbye, darling.'

Gaby shivered. Her mother was three hundred miles away; she couldn't possibly know what she was going through. It was one of those typical vague things her mother was always saying. It was like reading the horoscopes in the daily paper, she reminded herself—occasionally something could be made to fit!

Or maybe her mother was actually talking about the real, physical stuff they called weather! Who would know? she thought with fond exasperation, heading from the office to a quiet lounge.

She ordered a cup of coffee, then curled up in one of the big armchairs and opened the first book. Since she had taken her first flying test at the age of sixteen, she had studied continuously to upgrade her licence, so her eyes and mind responded to the textbook, seeking out the bits of information she wanted and storing them away.

Her mother had explained about her seizures to Gaby when she was seven, and she had a permanent picture in her mind of a brain like a fuse-box, and epilepsy as a short circuit kind of reaction in the fuses. 'Faulty wiring there', her mother had told her. Now she read that seizures could also be caused by metabolic disturbances, when the normal chemical environment of the brain cells was altered.

Could Jack have some underlying illness that was causing his faints?

And you think you can sit here in Wyndham and find a solution to something experts back in Boston couldn't find? her common sense mocked. Wouldn't underlying illness be the first thing the specialists would test?

She read through the prescribed blood tests that would rule out the different metabolic imbalances. Simple enough even for a lay person to comprehend, she decided. Of course the doctors in Boston would have done all those tests!

She ignored the cynical comments one part of her mind was making. All she wanted to do was find out more about epilepsy, and any other kind of seizure that might be included in Sue's books.

The International Classification of Epileptic Seizures caught her eye. She knew her mother sufferent complex partial seizures, and she read the description of these before returning to the classification. Atonic seizures, or drop attacks, would be the most likely scenario if Jack's fainting spells were epileptic, but there was little information about them in this book.

She sighed and put it down. The man was a doctor. He probably knew much more about his own health than these books would. Why had she wanted to read them? What business was it of hers anyway?

All the unanswerable questions trooped through her mind again. She would be better off sitting on the chair in her room, watching him sleep! Or maybe lying on the bed beside him. It was a huge bed, after all!

She sighed again and turned back to the books, growing more interested when she reached the section on electroencephalogram testing. The little waves made by the EEG reminded her of weather patterns, but the more she read, the less conclusive things became. Subjects having a seizure while undergoing an

EEG showed a definite pattern, and most patients showed enough significant abnormality in the EEG to have a diagnosis of epilepsy confirmed. But there was always a 'but', she realised, reading on. Not all persons tested by an EEG showed the interictal discharges that were typical of epilepsy.

Was Jack one of these people? Had he been tested and not shown any abnormality, so epilepsy had been discounted?

The questions nagged at her, although she could not have explained why. Whatever was wrong with the man was his problem, not hers, she reminded herself, but she could not escape the need to know more.

Was it something to do with the unhappiness she sensed within him? Did she think that, by sorting out his health, she could send him away happy?

Making Jack happy was not her job, she warned herself. None of her business! Nothing to do with her!

Someone came in and turned on lights and she looked up, startled to find that it had grown dark. Slipping the books back into their bag, she carried them back to her room, opening the door as noiselessly as possible. She crossed the dark room carefully and switched on the bathroom light.

It lightened the gloom in the bedroom as well. She peered across at Jack and decided he hadn't moved since she had left. She shoved the bag of books into the bottom òf the wardrobe, then sorted through the clothes for the dress she remembered seeing earlier.

Her mind told her Jack would not wake, but her wayward heart wanted to look her best—just in case.

'There's always Brian!' she told herself aloud, then felt a stab of guilt. By having dinner with him, was she encouraging him to think she was interested in him?

Couldn't she be interested in him?

She turned on the shower and stepped under the steaming water, her head shaking in reply to the silent question. One of the young doctors who had come to Derby on contract to the RFDS had shown a similar interest in her, and, lonely for companionship and eager for love, she had been tempted to indulge in a light-hearted flirtation with him.

Some deep-seated knowledge had told her he was not the man who would make her life complete, but other girls flirted, had boyfriends—affairs, even—so she had let herself be persuaded that it was all in fun.

Until the time had come for him to return to Perth! He had demanded that she return with him, declared that he loved her passionately and could not live without her, and nearly ruined both their lives with six months of unrelenting pursuit—phone calls, letters, newspaper advertisements, and flying visits back to Derby.

His dogged determination had frightened her, but his insistence that she must love him—why else had she gone out with him?—had left a worse scar, making her steer clear of any relationship, no matter how casual.

Brian will have to look after himself,' she told her reflection as she dressed. 'I'm going home tomorrow, so there's no time for him to get too attached.'

She tried to sound light-hearted, but she knew now that time had nothing to do with attraction. There were no minimum limits in this falling love business. She had seen a tense, tired man at an airport, and one momentary meeting of their eyes had changed her life so totally that she was finding it difficult to function normally

'Tomorrow he'll be gone—and until then probably

asleep!' She grimaced at her face, pale in the steamy bathroom. 'Mum could be wrong,' she assured herself, but the assurance failed to ease the panic she felt deep within her. Her mother's contention that somewhere in the world there was the 'one true, perfect love' for everyone had always comforted her. Now it was like a pronouncement of doom!

What if Jack was hers but hadn't known that simple fact—over there in America—when he'd married the ice-cool blonde?

'There must be more than one,' she argued with her absent mother. 'There *must* be!'

'Gaby?'

Had she woken him?

She darted out of the bathroom, but after the brightness her eyes were unable to adjust quickly, and she hovered uncertainly at the edge of the shaft of light.

'Not only clean but beautiful!' he murmured, his voice sounding drugged, the words slightly slurred.

She walked across to the bed, drawn inexorably towards him.

'You need more sleep,' she whispered as she sank down two body-widths away from him.

'That and other things,' he said, his voice so deep and husky that it vibrated against her flesh.

His hand reached out, and hers lifted to meet it.

'Food!' She forced the word out through lips that tingled with a burning need to brush across his skin. Her heart was going berserk in her chest, and her lungs had stopped working properly, but her mind clung desperately to one remaining shred of sanity. 'I'll bring some dinner in for you!'

'Only for me?'

He rolled over on to his side, bringing his body closer to where she perched so hesitantly. She used her concern to blot out the vibrant waves of sexual longing that his body was transmitting into hers.

'You have to eat,' she told him earnestly, spouting what she had been reading only hours earlier. 'You should always have regular meals, and regular sleep. Working too hard, missing meals, not getting enough sleep—all those things could have contributed to your fainting.'

'The most beautiful woman in the world is sitting on the side of my bed, and she's telling me I need to sleep and eat regularly,' he muttered. 'No one would believe this conversation!'

The strained note of cynicism had crept back into his voice, and she regretted her words.

'I care what happens to you,' she mumbled, letting her fingers move against his, gently imparting their own message.

'Do you, Gaby?' he asked. He gave her hand a sharp tug that destroyed her balance and brought the top half of her body toppling down on to the bed.

'If you care, then let me hold you for a moment,' he murmured, and his arms, not waiting for a reply, drew her close.

She nestled against him, drawing her legs up so that she was lying properly, and could feel his shape through the sheet that separated them.

'I've bought you some clothes. They're in the bags on the bench by the door if you want to check them later.'

She whispered the information against the skin beneath his ear, keeping her lips busy with talk so that they would not yield to the temptation to press kisses on the skin instead of words.

'Thank you, Gaby,' he said, thickly, his cheek moving against the silken heaviness of her clean hair.

His arms tightened, drawing her even closer, and her head rested on the pillow beside his. In the shadows, his eyes were too dark for colour, but she looked into them, knowing the blue so well that she fancied she could see it. He moved closer, kissed her lips, then moved fractionally away, still holding her body so close that she felt the tension leave his muscles as his body relaxed, and she knew he had fallen asleep again.

She lay still for what seemed like hours, not wanting to disturb him until he was sleeping deeply. Finally, judging the time was right, she lifted her head and leant forward to return his kiss, marvelling at the softness of his lips, the special magic of the taste of him. Then she lifted his arm from her shoulder and slid her body carefully off the bed.

She returned from a pleasant dinner, a left-over smile from Brian's light-hearted nonsense hovering about her lips. Jack was still sleeping, his breathing deep and even.

Trying to be as quiet as she could, she crept through to the bathroom again, leaving the plate of plastic-wrapped sandwiches she'd brought back for him on the top of the vanity unit. The darkness was so absolute, he would have to turn on the bathroom light if he was up during the night, and would see them there.

She crept out into the room and, fumbling in a leather folder, found a pen and paper. Back in the bathroom, she rejected 'Jack, here's some food' as unnecessarily abrupt, and nibbled on the end of the pen while she tried to word what she wanted to say. 'I love you, have a sandwich' would be shockingly forward, while 'Thought you might be hungry' seemed too casual. In the end, she settled on a formal note that read:

Dear Jack,
   Thought you might be hungry, but please don't sit in the bathroom to eat. Turn on the light in the bedroom and get yourself a cup of tea or coffee. You won't disturb me.

As she sighed 'Gaby' at the end of it, she thought about crossing out the last ambiguity. She could have said, You disturb me so much already, what's a little more disruption?

She prepared for bed, unduly pleased that the night-dress provided by K's Fashions was a smooth cream satin with a heavy lace trim that stretched across her breasts.

She tiptoed across the room, her heart pounding so heavily, she held her breath, wondering what on earth she could say if he woke up and found her getting into bed with him.

She felt his hand feeling across the bed, reaching her shoulder, pausing for a moment. Then he gripped her and pulled her close. Little contented, snuffling noises told her he was still asleep. Common sense told her he was reaching for Lauren, but a sense of impending loss made her slip closer to him, curving her body into the concave arc of his and relaxing into the warm security of his grasp.

CHAPTER EIGHT

'Up, up, up, miss!'

Her father's habitual wake-up call dragged Gaby from the depths of sleep. Her back felt cold, and a quick exploration with one hand told her she was alone in the big bed. She sat up and shook her head, hoping to clear it of the delusion that her father, not Jack Fletcher, was in the room.

She blinked and looked again, but it was definitely her father, impatience radiating out of every pore as he strode about the unit gathering up clothes and shoving them into carrier bags.

'Come on, Gaby. It's a bright and beautiful day, but you know darned well, after rain like we've had, a bit of heat will bring on thunderstorms. I want to be back home by lunchtime.'

She blinked again and shook herself, checking that it wasn't a dream.

'Into the shower with you. Breakfast will be here any minute. Want some of these clothes to put on?'

She clambered off the bed, took the carrier bags from his outstretched hand and hurried away, shutting the bathroom door and leaning weakly against it.

An empty plate confronted her, and the note tucked under it read, 'Thanks.'

Thanks! That was all he had to say? Her mind yelled the words, and she turned on the shower, needing its noise to drown out the rage that forced a string of unflattering adjectives on to her lips. This man had walked into her life, disrupted it totally, and left an empty plate and a note saying 'thanks'.

She was glad, she told herself. At least being angry with him was keeping the devastation that lurked beneath the anger at bay. As she dressed, she remembered pulling on the delicate, feminine nightdress, remembered preening—just a little—in front of the mirror, and another emotion surfaced.

She had climbed into his bed, provocatively clad, and pressed her body into his! Shame brought her blood back to boiling-poing, searing her cheeks with vivid evidence of her embarrassment.

Her unspoken acquiescence, her moving into his arms, had been as good as offering herself to him, and walking out was his reply—his rejection!

She heard breakfast trays arriving and splashed cool water on her face. As she re-entered the bedroom, she realised that the bags with the clothes she'd bought for him were also gone, and didn't know whether to feel angrier or relieved.

Her father was fussing over breakfast, setting the small table with the deliberation he brought to all tasks.

'There,' he said, when all was arranged to his satisfaction. 'Now let's look at you! None the worse for your adventure?'

He held her at arm's length for a moment, then drew her close into a warm embrace.

'Were you worried?' he asked as they sat down to eat.

'Worried about you worrying,' she told him, smiling at him as her world still rocked from the upheaval Jack had caused. At least her father—indeed her whole family—was a point of stability!

'Would you make the same decision again?'

It was the question she had asked herself a hundred times! The question she's hadn't, up until now, got around to answering.

'I think so. . .' she said slowly, wondering how much he knew. Everything, knowing her father! 'The fellow's burns were bad, but not, at the time, life-threatening, but the heart attack would have killed him. We were at least eighty minutes out of Derby, possibly more as we were flying into head-winds. Once we were on the ground he could be stabilised and his condition watched. There were drugs in Carole's bag to treat him.'

She shrugged uneasily as she finished explaining, still not one hundred per cent certain she had made the correct decision.,

'I think you did the right thing, and so does that doctor fellow you had in the plane.'

Gaby's head shot up as her father pronounced his judgement. Where and when had he spoken to Jack? When had her father arrived? Had it been early enough to walk into the room and find her asleep in a stranger's arms? Was that why Jack had left so abruptly.

The questions beat into her brain, but they were not the kind of things she could ask her father. She squirmed uneasily in her seat, poking at the bacon and eggs he considered an indispensable part of breakfast.

Peering up under her eyelashes, she looked at him, but could see no trace of reproach or disappointment in his face nor feel any disapproval in his demeanour.

'They're sending the bloke straight through to Perth. One of your Derby planes is due up shortly, and they'll collect him, then stop in Broome to pick up a fellow who was badly injured when his semi-trailer was rolled over by the wind between Derby and Broome, and take them both south.'

If I ask about Jack's place in all these plans, it will bring up the subject I'd just as soon avoid with my father, she realised, and clamped her lips shut on the question that hovered there.

'We might see them at the airport,' she said as casually as she could. 'Does the base know I'm going back home with you?'

He stopped spreading marmalade on his toast for long enough to nod.

'I've been on to them. Mike said you had three days off due to you, then a three-day stand-by shift, then three days off for Christmas. I told him I'd pick up Fred in Derby then fly you both back to the abandoned strip if he wanted you to fly the Cessna back.'

Her father's pre-occupation with food had suddenly ceased, and his full attention was focused on her.

'Worried if I don't get back on to the horse after a fall I might never ride again?' she asked, a smile finally breaking through her depression.

'Not really,' he muttered, as if embarrassed to be caught worrying about her dedication. 'You've always been a spunky kid. I'd never doubt your courage.'

He pushed his plate away, his uneasiness communicating itself to her. This was the perfect opening for her father to point out the folly of her ways—to deliver yet another lecture on her chosen career.

'But?' she asked, puzzled by what could be bothering him.

'Your mother thought you were hurt! All right, but hurt! She was uneasy earlier, before I saw you in Broome.' The words burst out with a kind of reluctance. Like her, he hated to be seen believing in her mother's intuitive sense, yet some of her pronouncements had been close enough for all members of the family to treat them warily. And now this!

Here she was, hurting like she'd never hurt before, and her mother had known! She shivered.

'Come on, Dad. Let's get out of this place. Mum's fortune-telling always did give us both the creeps.'

The day was unbelievably bright and beautiful, the air fresh and sweet, the buildings cleansed of their usual covering of dust and green grass already sprouting from the red earth. Far to the east, a band of cloud marked Elvie's progress inland, and Gaby wondered if it would still be raining when they reached home.

At the airport the big army helicopter stood deserted, and the RFDS plane was landing.

'Let's go, Dad,' Gaby urged, not wanting to have to cope with the teasting banter from a fellow pilot, nor risk seeing the man who had said his thanks already.

He was already gone from her life. All she had to do was get over him—to seal the memory of that tiny period of time away in her mind and heart forever.

'Want to take her home?'

Her father always asked, and usually she accepted his offer with excitement. The little Piper was a joy to fly.

'Not today, Dad, although I will get back on that damned horse.'

Three days of normality—Sam's teasing, the stockmen's jokes, her mother's absent-minded affection—restored most of her equanimity, and although her heart still ached when she climbed into bed each evening, and her mind still churned with impossible dreams, she was reasonably certain that no one knew.

'You'll be back on Christmas Eve, Dad says.' Her mother hugged her goodbye on the morning of her departure. 'I think the fellow's coming the day before that,' she added. 'Dad's taking Sam's friend back to Broome that day.'

'Come on, Sis,' Sam called impatiently. He was anxious to get into the air and handle the controls. She kissed her mother quickly, remembering her own impatience at the same age. She'd ring and ask about 'the fellow' if she remembered, although her parents were forever picking up stray people and inviting them to stay.

The chartered Cessna was on the tarmac when they landed in Derby. Someone had flown her back already! She waved farewell to the family. Sam had insisted that they fly home via the strip where she had landed so that he could check out the cave and show his friend where the little drama had been played out.

She watched the Piper lift into the sky and wished she were still with them. The idea of work had lost its gloss of excitement, although she knew that was nothing to do with the accident. It was because the job which she had considered the primary force in her life had been superseded in importance by something as ephemeral—and unsatisfactory—as love, and every moment was a little longer, a little flatter and a little less joyful because it was unshared.

The town looked scarred, but the clean-up crews had restored order, and the bright sun had encouraged the inhabitants to make the most of the fine weather. Carpets and floor rugs lay across veranda railings, or were spread like multi-coloured grass in front yards. Behind the houses, on every clothes-line, washing hung like bright flags of victory. Nature had done its worst, but the town had survived its onslaught.

Gaby reported to the base, where her first morning was spent compiling a detailed report of her adventurous trip. She learned that Carole, with Bernie's family, had arrived back in Derby the previous afternoon, having sat out the bad weather at a property off the Gibb River road. Bernie's wife and children had travelled on to Perth, driven by a sensible uncle who had arrived to take care of them.

So all the ends were nicely tied up, she thought—but no one had mentioned Jack. Did they assume she knew what had happened to him? Or think she wasn't interested?

She discovered that he had returned to Broome on the flight that took Bernie south. The plane's manifest, neatly filed next to her own report, had told her that much.

And I'm left here, with a mass of information I never needed to know about epilepsy in my head, and a hollow place in my heart which I know will never be filled.

She smiled and laughed and joked with a determination that left her exhausted at the end of each day. Flying to Kalumburu to bring out a young aboriginal girl who had developed complications during her first pregnancy, she flew over the old airstrip and looked down. For a moment, panic clutched at her heart.

It wasn't fear of flying, but fear of a life of loneliness as she finally confronted the fact that she would never see him again

She piloted the Piper home on Christmas Eve. She had learnt that keeping busy was good! It gave her less time for unprofitable speculation, fewer moments to add up her savings and speculate on the chances of coincidence taking a hand if she happened to go to America on her holidays and visit Boston as part of her trip. And that was only one of the many wild, illogical schemes that kept her mind active when she longed for the oblivion of sleep!

From the cockpit, she surveyed the familiar country, curiously changed by the wide brown stretches of water that streamed across it, and the green of fresh grass pushing through the heat-baked earth.

'If the wet keeps up like this, it'll be a good season,' she remarked to her father, then smiled as Sam broke into the conversation, explaining all they planned to do at Teralga if the dams were filled and they had plenty of good feed once again.

She let him rattle on, knowing she had probably sounded the same at his age and remembering the pride she'd felt at being included in her father's discussions about the season.

Discussion had turned to argument by the time the little plane kissed the hard all-weather surface of the Teralga strip. Gaby ignored the talk and taxied towards a waiting vehicle.

The solid figure in stockman's gear and wide-brimmed hat climbed down from the old Land Rover they used around the property and stood, one arm raised to shade his eyes, as she taxied to a halt.

Is my heart going to react like this every time I see someone the same shape as Jack? she wondered, trying to work out which of the men had come to meet them.

Her father climbed out, then Sam, and she followed, savouring the feeling of coming home for a moment before she left the plane.

'Hello, Gaby!' the deep voice said, and her knees buckled as her feet hit the ground. He was there to catch her, reaching out and gripping her arm with one hand, steadying her as she found her balance.

'What are you doing here?' she whispered, sheer bewilderment settling like fog in her brain.

'You didn't know I'd be here?' He sounded as astonished by that information as she was by his presence. 'But your father asked me when I met him in Wyndham. I was on my way over to the hospital to check on Bernie when he arrived. We got talking about all that had happened, and somehow we hit it off. He said, "What about coming out over Christmas to see a bit of real Australia?" and here I am.

He smiled at her. Her heart did its flipping trick, and the fireworks started in her blood, but her mind held her rooted to the stop, telling her to get back on the plane, fly back to Derby—anywhere!—because seeing Jack with Lauren was going to be more than she could handle.

'Aren't you pleased?'

The strained note had crept into his voice and she looked up quickly into his eyes, seeing anxiety and something else that baffled her in their blueness.

'I. . . You surprised me!' she finished, calling up all her reserves of strength to carry this through. 'Mum said a "fellow" was coming for Christmas. I didn't think about it being you.'

The words stumbled out, falling over each other in her effort to sound composed—to make sense!

She realised she was still standing where she had landed when she dropped from the plane, while her father and Sam were doing all the unloading.

And where were you when you met my father? she wanted to ask. Inside my bedroom or somewhere else?

It was her first rational thought since she'd seen him, but instead of being pleased that her mind was returning to normal it annoyed her. She couldn't ask it anyway. And why was it suddenly so important?

'I'm sorry I didn't see you to say goodby in Wyndham,' he murmured, stepping away from her and reaching into the hold of the plane to help lift out the last-minute Christmas shopping she had done for her mother, and the box of brightly wrapped gifts she'd brought home. His voice had that huskiness that reverberated through to her toes, and she stared at him, puzzled by what she thought she could hear in it. He put down one box at her feet, then leaned into the plane again. 'Getting out of that bed was the hardest thing I ever did,' he added, the words muffled by his shirt as they filtered back to her across his shoulder. He straightened again, and turned to her, his arms holding the last box. 'And coming here could well have been the stupidest.'

But his eyes, though full of shadows, are telling me he loves me.

The certainty of this revelation struck her like a lightning bolt. She bent down, picked up the box he'd put down earlier and walked swiftly over to the Land Rover where her father and brother continued their heated argument about the relative merits of different cattle breeds.

'Young bull and old bull!' Gaby muttered as she joined them. Still arguing, Sam turned to take her parcel while her father packed the one Jack carried into the back of the vehicle.

Sam slid behind the wheel, and, as her father always

travelled in the front passenger seat when he wasn't driving, it left Gaby and Jack to share the back. She held herself stiffly as Sam careered down the road that led to the homestead, grabbing at the window to stop herself being lurches against the man who occupied all her thoughts.

Her mother waited on the wide veranda, a slim figure in blue merging with the shadows from the grape-vines that festooned the house and provided welcome shade in summer.

'Happy, darling?' her mother asked as she hugged her in welcome. She smiled, a warm but secretive smile that hinted at conspiracy.

Really! Gaby thought exasperatedly. For someone who's supposed to be tuned in to the thoughts and feelings of her family, Mum's missed the mark this time.

She returned the hug then walked down the long, cool corridor towards her bedroom. As she nudged open the door, she realised that Jack was close behind her, carrying her small bag and the box of presents.

'Where's Lauren?' she croaked, determined to end the farce before it went any further.

He stood in the doorway, as if the question had put up an invisible barrier between them.

'She went back to the States!'

Six words that told her nothing except that Lauren was not here, and she would not have to bear the pain of seeing them together. A tiny bud of hope began to openin her breast.

'Why did you come?'

'Because I had to see you again.' With this flat statement he took a wary step forward. 'Selfish of me, wasn't it?' His lips twisted into a bitter smile.

'Especially when I'm the reason this attraction between us can go no further.'

Gaby watched his shoulders lift in a helpless shrug. *Him* helpless? What was *she* supposed to say to that?

Before anything she might usefully reply came into her head, he was speaking again.

'Even after I accepted the invitation I knew I should phone and say I couldn't make it! Knew I should get as far away as I could, as fast as I could, but I couldn't do it. I found I had to see you again, even if only to take the memory of a few happy days together with me into an uncertain future on the other side of the world.'

Gaby sank on to the bed as she absorbed this information. She understood exactly what he had felt. Forgetting the rights or wrongs of the situation, she could understand this desire to steal a little packet of happiness. Her own excitement—her agitated pulse and pounding heart—told her she felt the same way.

She fought the treacherous thoughts, searching for a neutral comment that might cut through the invisible threads pulling them together and set her free—for a little time, at least.

'Maybe a holiday will help your fainting spells.' Not the best subject to bring up, she decided immediately the words were out, but a practical one!

He remained one step into the room, holding the box and her bag, and shook his head.

'The only thing that could help would be a diagnosis of some kind,' he said in the strained voice that hurt her when she heard it. 'Although crash-landings in a cyclone and a night of survival medicine hasn't done any harm. I've been free of the stupid turns since you dumped us in the bush.'

He smiled at her, and the tenderness in his

expression reached across the room like a physical force, enfolding her in a warmth that brought her body back to tingling, vibrant life.

'You'd better put Gaby's gear down before you turn to stone,' Sam told him, loping through the door and reaching over Jack's shoulder to rifle through the presents. 'Which one's mine, Sis?' he asked. 'Let's have a feel.'

He took the box and tipped it on the bed, and Gaby slapped at his hands, trying to keep his gangly limbs away from the glittering piles.

'Come on, Jack! Look for yours! Sam urged the visitor, but Jack just smiled at the sibling tussle and walked away.

He seemed to have fitted into her family so easily, she thought when she walked into her mother's studio a little later and saw him perched on the wide work-bench, his strong, capable hands tenderly sorting through the tiny charms her mother crafted with delicate precision.

'Not all visitors are allowed in here,' she remarked, wandering over to examine the chain links her mother was shaping.

'I'm being useful,' he told her with a smile that stole her breath away.

'He's peaceful,' her mother explained. 'Although there's plenty of agitation boiling around inside him, at the moment he's at ease.'

Gaby slanted a glance from the woman to the man, but Jack showed no surprise at hearing such a strange pronouncement, and her mother showed no indication that she was making a particular point.

'But you'll have to go, Gaby,' her mother added. 'You're too fidgety to be in here today. You've time for a ride before lunch. Your father had a few horses brought in for Sam and his mate. They've been riding each day so the animals won't be overly fresh.'

'I can ride,' Jack offered, and something beneath the words asked for an invitation.

'Come on, then,' Gaby said, beckoning towards the door with her head. 'Let's see.'

She smiled, forgetting everything but the promise of pleasure. To ride across the paddocks of her beloved Teralga with this man by her side was like being given a dream.

Sam was tinkering with his motorbike over by the yards, and he offered to help saddle up.

'Help Jack,' she said. 'I'll slip back to the house and change into jeans.'

She went via the kitchen, hugging Nell, their cook-housekeeper, as she went through.

'I'm taking Jack for a ride. Could we take a sandwich lunch?' An appealing grin accompanied the question. Nell was known to become quite volubly upset when people missed her meals.

'Just this once, I suppose,' she said grudgingly, but the smile that accompanied the words told Gaby she was happy for her.

Once changed, Gaby collected their lunch, packed, with drinks and fruit, into a small backpack, and hurried back to the yards.

Jack sat easily on a solid bay horse that her father sometimes rode when time and the pressure of work allowed him a quiet day. Sam had saddled a bright chestnut gelding for her, and he snickered quietly as she rubbed his muzzle.

'Not coming yourself, Sam?' Jack asked.

As Sam shook his head and turned back towards his

bike, Gaby explained, 'If he's been riding lately, it's because his mate enjoyed it. Horses are far too slow for Sam. He's a modern man!'

She lifted herself into the saddle and smiled at Jack.

'I used to think I was one of them,' he said, then turned and looked around the flat red plains towards the mountains, purple in the distance. 'But here, in wild west kind of country, I feel curiously at home.'

You look quite at home, too, she would have liked to tell him as her heart swelled with happiness to see him so relaxed in her environment.

'We'll see if you still feel that way after a few hours in the saddle,' she said instead, and led the way across the home paddocks and on to the track that would take them to the foothills of the range.

As they rode, side by side, the rhythmic movement of the horse beneath her and the sweet smell of the dust-free air filled Gaby with an ease she had not felt for a long time. She pointed out different trees, explained about bores, described the scene at muster-time, when mobs of cattle moved through the red dust like an animated mirage. Imperceptibly, her mind and body relaxed, and she allowed the sheer delight of the day and the special thrill of this man's company to creep into her heart.

They halted the horses in a sheltered glade at the bottom of a sheer cliff. Water fell with a white joyousness from a cleft at the top to a deep pool, then flowed out along a depression that only a week ago had been a dry gully.

'Do you swim here?' Jack asked, without turning to look at her.

'Not yet,' she told him. 'That was the first big rain of the season, and the water will be full of sticks and rubbish that has collected in the dry creek beds all year. By the end of the wet, about March or April, the hole will be clear and safe.'

He turned round and looked at her, and she knew he was telling her that he would not see it like that.

'It's a good place for lunch,' she added as the pain started again, spoiling her bright, beautiful day.

He swung easily off his horse, surprising her, as he always did, with his perfect pysical co-ordination. She lifted her leg over the saddle and as she slid to the ground he caught her, turning her in his arms and bending to kiss her in the same smooth movement.

She responded with all the heat and passion of a body starved for love, leaning into his muscular chest, while her lips pressed harder and harder, trying to slake the thirst for him that was firing her body and tormenting her soul.

As his lips opened and his tongue teased at the contours of her mouth the fireworks exploded again in her blood and she opened her mouth to taste him, trembling with the urgency of her need.

'Sweet, beautiful Gaby!' he murmured. 'Most precious of people!'

The words might have been imagined, but she felt his lips moving against hers and knew they were real.

'I have nothing to offer you, my love.' He pressed a kiss against each eyelid. 'No future, Gaby, do you understand?' Now his lips fluttered on the skin beneath her ear, her chin, and down her neck. 'But there is today, and tomorrow, and the next day.' The lips moved back to claim hers, as if he feared she might argue with his feverish warnings and he did not want to hear what she might say!

She slid her arms around his neck and held him

close, trying to tell him with her kisses that this moment was all that mattered—that now might last forever!

As he returned her kiss with a fervour that told her he understood, she found her body tingling with the awakening desire that his touch had engendered once before.

Three days, they had. Long enough for a love-affair?

Her fingers curled into the thick dark hair, gripping at its wiry strength as if it could provide some answers to her dilemma.

Would happiness—even one small parcel of it—stolen from someone else's life, remain, or would guilt tarnish the shining wonder of it?

Her body throbbed its response to his, crying out for all the unknown splendour that she knew only he could provide

'Perhaps we should tether your horse,' he muttered, raising his head and gazing blankly at the patient animal who stood behind her. As he lifted the reins from her fingers, she realised they must have been dangling round his head while she'd clung to his hair.

'One more move and I might have strangled you,' she responded, wondering if that was why he'd stopped.

She pushed herself away from his body, searching his face for some clue to what he might be thinking. It was set, closed against her, but as she watched he glance down and the blue, blue eyes met hers—full of love and shadows once again.

CHAPTER NINE

THEY sat close together on a fallen log, eating the lunch that Nell had prepared. Their arms brushed against each other as they moved, and it seemed to Gaby that they moved and breathed as one. Even her heart must be beating in time to his, she decided as the feeling of completeness settled over her like a precious fragrance.

Occasionally he asked a question, about a bird once, then the wallaby that hopped into the clearing, stood for a moment surveying them with wide brown eyes, then hopped, unhurriedly away.

As she answered she used the words that anyone would use, but, in the same way as his questions had masked the need for reassurance about her feelings, her replies revealed her love in every nuance of her voice.

'There's an old aboriginal legend about a day when time stood still, so twenty-four hours became a life-time,' she whispered when the purple colour of the hills deepened to indigo shadows.

'And similar stories in every culture, I would think. My mother used to talk about an old musical set in Scotland called *Brigadoon*, and there's that American film called *Groundhog Day* about a lifetime in a day. Would you like today to last forever?'

She turned to him and studied his face. His tilted eyebrows and half-smile asked the question, but the lack of little laughter-lines fanning out from his eyes told her he was serious.

'Can't it?' she asked, although she didn't believe in that kind of magic.

'I can't see how it can, Gaby!' he replied in a voice that pleaded for her understanding.

There's such a thing as divorce, she thought, but she knew now was not the time to bring that up. He had known her for precisely a week, and most of that time had been spent apart. How could he break up a marriage that probably had its roots in his childhood—between two people from the same background, culture and country—for a virtual stranger?

'Don't look so sad,' he murmured, leaning towards her to brush his lips across hers so lightly that it was like the touch of thistledown.

The touch brought her nerves to clamouring life again, and an almost soundless cry escaped on a breath of air, before his lips settled more firmly. She felt his hand against her hair, pressing her head to his, while his fingers wound through the silky strands. With a sigh, she surrendered herself to the special joy of being in his arms, to the bliss of the kisses he pressed on her lips, and the excitement of this hands moving on her body.

'Will you family think we're lost?'

Gaby snuggled deeper into his arms, marvelling at the compact strength of his body, then opened her eyes to face the fact that the sun had disappeared behind the hills.

'Probably,' she replied, stretching up to press her lips to his once again.

'Then we should go back,' he told her, between

little, puckered, teasing, silly kisses that made her want to laugh and cry at the same time.

They rode with a reluctance that the horses must have sensed, plodding back through the twilight to the low, rambling old homestead. For the first time in her life Gaby failed to feel the sudden spurt of happiness that coming home had always elicited. For coming home today meant other people, and the thought of sharing Jack's company, even with her beloved family, was causing her a great deal of mental turmoil.

One of the stockmen met them at the yards and offered to unsaddle and rub down the horses.

'No argument today?' he asked in surprise when Gaby calmly handed over her reins. She shook her head, smiled at him and walked away, too lost in her own distracting thoughts to insist on looking after the horses herself.

Jack followed her back towards the house, but they did not speak. The touch of his lips still lingered on her skin, the man smell of him still teased in her nostrils.

'I'll see you at dinner,' he murmured. The deep voice seemed to slide directly into her blood, sending it rioting through her veins once again.

Back in her room, she sank on to the bed, knowing she had to hurry to shower and change before joining the family on the veranda for a drink before dinner.

Slowly, she rubbed her hands up and down her arms, feeling the skin that he had touched, trying to imagine how it had felt to him. His had felt surprisingly cool, considering the heat of the day, and the tempestuous kisses.

She closed her eyes and felt his lips touch hers, and her body curled into itself as she remembered delight sparkled along her nerves to the centre of her womanhood. She hugged herself, reliving the pleasure, and smiled.

'You decent, Sis?' Sam's voice boomed through her door.

'Five minutes,' she promised, and dashed into the bathroom, peeling off her jeans as she went.

He was on her bed, lifting all the Christmas presents and weighing them in his hands, as she emerged in her underwear.

'Nice fella, that Jack,' he said casually, and Gaby peered intently at him. Her Scrappy *was* growing up if he was taking an interest in her love life!

'Stop fiddling with those parcels and tell me what to wear,' she ordered, not wanting to take his tentative opening any further.

'Wear that red thing Dad brought back from Perth for Mum but it didn't fit her,' he said without hesitating, and Gaby pulled out the red linen sheath.

Festive enough for Christmas Eve, she decided, slipping it over her head then backing towards Sam so that he could zip it up for her. He did it awkwardly, then hovered behind her for a moment, before heading for the door.

'I wouldn't like you to go too far away,' he said, throwing the words over his shoulder as he walked out into the passage and shut the door behind him.

'You don't have to worry,' she murmured into the air, realising for the first time that maybe it was a good thing Jack was married and would soon be on his way back to where he belonged. She didn't think she could have transplanted to that cold northern climate if he had been free to offer her his love.

The thought of being so far from Teralga and her

family made her shiver, but it brought her mind out of the foolish dreams and back into focus.

Until she stepped out on to the veranda!

'He was perched on the railing, a beer in his hand, looking as much at home in her world as her father and Sam did. She paused in the doorway, drinking in the scene, distilling it like some rare essence into her mind.

He was talking quietly to her mother, his head bent low towards her. He was relaxed, she realised as her body's antennaes failed to pick up the tension she had felt emanating from his body when they'd first met.

'Drink, Gaby?' her father asked, while she was still marvelling at this new dimension of Jack Fletcher.

'Soda water and ice,' she replied, knowing this was not a night for confusing even one of her brain cells with alcohol.

'Jack's been telling us about an operation surgeons are performing in the United States to relieve some people of epileptic seizures,' her father explained.

Gaby choked on her first mouthful of soda water, coughing and spluttering helplessly while this new shock rattled through her system. Her mother never spoke to outsiders about her illness—never, never, never! It was an inviolate rule of the house, and here she was chatting to this stranger about possible operations.

And what of Jack? He must suspect epilepsy in his own case! How did he feel having the matter discussed in a family conclave?

She gazed at the pair in total incomprehension until they turned together and smiled at her—welcoming smiles, as if she was the outsider! Was the world going mad? Hers was certainly turning upside-down several times a day!

She swung away from their smiles, sinking down on to the arm of her father's canvas and wood chair. He and Sam were caught in a heated discussion of trail bikes.

'Do you two ever agree on anything?' she asked when a break in their argument allowed her to get a word in.

'No!' they replied in unison, they laughed uproariously at their own feeble joke.

Gaby smiled, but still felt excluded. Jack Fletcher had only been at her home for one full day, so why did he seem so at ease, and she feel like the odd one out?

'Jack is going to get some information for us from the States, and find out if similar work is being done in Australia.' Her father stopped arguing with Sam for long enough to tell her more about the other conversation. 'It seems that people with your mother's type of seizures are good candidates for the operation——'

'Only if the focus of the seizure is in the anterior temporal lobe, or the inferior frontal region of the cortex,' Jack interrupted, warning them not to let their hopes leap ahead of common sense. 'Both of those regions can be excised without causing neurological damage that will affect other functions.

'But Mum's seizures are well-controlled through medication,' Gaby argued, 'as long as she's sensible about getting plenty of sleep and eating regularly. Isn't any head operation a risk?'

'Her heart was beating furiously. Because she was concerned about her mother, or because Jack had smiled at her?

He nodded his agreement gravely, then smiled again. 'The risks are less than average for surgery,' he assured them all, 'but the success-rates aren't all that good either. I think, from memory, there's about a thirty to forty per cent chance of being seizure-free for several years, and another thirty or forth per cent chance of gaining considerable relief for a few years, but that still leaves about twenty per cent who get no relief.'

'Not worth the trauma of an operation, I would say'

Gaby was watching her mother when her father made this pronouncement, and was surprised by the shadow of disappointment that clouded the beautiful face for a moment. Her mother had always seemed so philosophical about her problem. Did it worry her more than she let her family suspect?

Sam was speaking to Jack now, asking why and how with all a teenager's avidity for bizarre technical knowledge.

Gaby listened absently to Jack's explanations of the delicate brain surgery while her mind puzzled over her mother's reaction. She was pleased when Nell appeared to call them in to dinner, and followed her thankfully out to the kitchen to help carry the food through to the dining-room.

Nell joined them for dinner, and as Gaby watched Jack pull out a chair for the older woman she marvelled again at his seeming acceptance by her normally reserved family. Once again, she felt the odd one out. If things had been different, would she still have resented the openness with which they had welcomed this man—or been pleased by it?

He's married, she wanted to shout at these well-meaning people, then realised that his marriage did not preclude him being their friend; it only precluded her from being anything more than a friend.

They moved back to the cool veranda for coffee, the cicadas providing their familiar background music to the desultory conversation that ranged from science to cattle then turned inevitably to the weather and finally star-gazing.

'You've seen the Southern Cross, I suppose?' Sam asked Jack, and when he shook his head they all cried shame, that he could have been in Australia for two months and not sought out the symbol of the country.

'Come one, I'll show you,' Sam said, but his mother put a hand on his arm and shook her head.

'Let Gaby show Jack the stars, Sam. Last time they spent a night together, all they saw were clouds and rain.'

Sam shrugged and walked inside, and Gaby wanted to follow him, to soothe the disquiet she knew he was feeling, but hiding her own tumult was taking all her strength and she had nothing left to offer her much loved brother.

Jack walked beside her down the two wide steps, his body assaulting hers with silent messages. She led the way through the garden that grew green and lush around the homestead, away from the lights of the house so that the stars would shine more brightly down on them.

'It's a magical night,' Jack murmured, reaching out to catch hold of her hand and draw her close by his side. 'A night for lovers!'

He spoke so easily of love and beauty, she thought, remembering other words he's whispered to her in the dark. Would her father have talked like that to her mother? Had Jack spoken this way to Lauren?

She squeezed his hand as pain shot through her. Her mother must be wrong. There had to be a hundred men with whom she'd feel the special magic! There *had* to be!

With a desperation born of her thought, she turned to him and stood on tiptoe, pressing her mouth against his, seeking the one certain way to blot out her thoughts.

'We're supposed to be looking at stars,' he muttered against her greedy lips while his arms locked around her back and held her tightly.

'I am,' she whispered back. 'Stars and sparklers and sky rockets everywhere!'

They swayed under the night sky as their limbs entwined in the embrace, lips giving and receiving promises they both knew would never be fulfilled.

'This is folly, Gaby!' he said at last, pushing her away from him and breathing deeply. 'I cannot offer you a part-person!'

The phrase rang oddly in her ears. Did he mean that the other part belonged to Lauren?

'That's the Southern Cross, up there.' Her voice was raw with the pain of tears denied release, and she stepped back from him as she pointed upwards to where the two pointers marked the cross that the old sailors had sought when they'd ventured into unmapped southern oceans.

She stared at the familiar stars, wishing with a futile anguish that they could guide her through this uncharted territory her heart had entered.

'I'm going in,' she said abruptly, then turned and hurried back to the safety of the house, praying that its familiarity would banish the desolation in her soul.

She woke to carols playing softly somewhere and lay, listening. The music came from the studio, she decided, and slipped out of bed, showered quickly and pulled on the white shorts and top her father had ordered for her in Wyndham.

Her mother's head was bent across the bench, half her face hidden behind her mask as she bent over the tiny flame of her gas burner.

'I want something special for Jack for Christmas,' she blurted out, and saw the dark head nod.

'I'm working on it now,' her mother said. 'Sit quietly for a few minutes. It will do you good.'

Gaby slumped on to a stool and waited, letting the old familiar songs work their magic on her troubled spirits.

Sam went off on his bike!' her mother said, her head still bent over her work.

'On Christmas Day? Without unwrapping his presents? Not like Sam!' Gaby joked, but when her mother didn't smile in response she added brusquely, 'There's no need for him to worry. I am not going off to American with Dad's visitor!'

Because he's married, she could have added, but she didn't want to hurt her family by betraying his secret.

'There are so many ways things can be worked out if one only takes the time and trouble to consider all options,; her mother said, but Gaby could make no sense of the words. 'I've finished,' she added. 'Look!'

She slid the finished piece across the bench towards Gaby, who reached out and ran her fingers over the dark red lump of semi-precious stone.

'Red jasper?' she asked, and her mother nodded, smiling with pride as she too looked at the heavy ornament.

Set in it were five silver stars in the unique formation of the Southern Cross, so finely wrought that they looked like pin-points of light in the natural grain of the jasper.

'It's beautiful, Mum! Thanks.'

Gaby leaned forward to kiss her mother's cheek, holding back the tears that sprang up from nowhere, filling her eyes and tightening her throat.

They walked together to the house, and Gaby wrapped Jack's present. The two men had gone off earlier, Nell informed them, without more than a cup of tea and some toast.

'And Sam had no breakfast,' she grumbled. 'Fine goings-on for Christmas Day, I must say!'

Gaby made coffee for her mother and herself, and more toast.

'You should be pleased no one wants a big cooked breakfast,' she said. 'You'll be busy enough doing lunch.'

And I could get on with it if you'd all get out of my kitchen and give me some peace,' Nell scolded, waving Gaby out with a flick of a tea-towel.

The men returned at eleven, but there was still no sign of Sam, and Gaby's unease grew with every minute he did not appear, even dimming her delight in having Jack close to her again.

'Wretched boy!' her father muttered, placing up and down the veranda and staring out over the plain for sight of a small cloud of dust.

The three stockmen who had stayed for Christmas walked up from their quarters, ready for the traditional Christmas dinner at the homestead, but they were greeted absent-mindedly.

'I'll take the Ultra-light up and see if I can see him!' James announced as lunchtime grew nearer. 'If you three could take the other bikes, and Jack and Gaby take the Land Rover, we can stay in touch on the two-ways. If I spot him and he's in trouble, I'll guide the nearest of you to him.'

He's sending Jack because he knows Sam would only be this late if he's had an accident, Gaby thought, panic spurting to life inside her.

Her mind listened to her father's directions, which way they were to drive, and when they were to turn back, but her heart was pleading with the fates to let her Scrappy be all right, to not let him suffer because she had lost her silly heart.

'We'll find him, Gaby,' Jack assured her, taking her arm and guiding her faltering footsteps towards the vehicle. 'Don't go to pieces now, when I need you to tell me where the Ten Mile is and work the two-way. Not stuff I'm used to doing back in Boston, you know.'

He's talking to make me feel better, she realised, hurrying beside him while his voice washed over and around her.

'Which direction?' he asked as he fired the engine, and she waved her hand towards the track that led out to the old bore.

'I'll drive slowly; you watch your side and I'll watch mine, and if we see anything that looks at all suspicious we'll leave the track and investigate, OK?'

'Thanks, Jack!' she managed to blurt out, then felt his hand patting her on the arm.

'You get the two-way operative,' was all he said, but his smile lit up the darkness that had gathered inside her.

They had driven about four miles before her father's voice crackled over the radio.

'He's your way, Gaby. About a mile short of the old bore south-east of your road. He's come off the bike but he's waving, so he's OK. You three on the bikes, head back home. I'm going down!'

Relief flowed over her, leaving a stomach-clenching nausea in its wake.

'You OK?' Jack asked.

'I will be,' she told him, wrapping her arms tightly around her body and rocking herself back and forth in the seat.

'Do I keep following this track?' he asked.

She forced herself to look around her, picking out the familiar landmarks and thinking of the fastest way to the spot her father had mentioned.

'To the next gate, then we'll turn and follow the fence. The old bore is about five miles down that paddock.'

They left the track and bounced along over the ground, baked hard again by the hot, dry days that had followed the cyclone. From a distance the little Ultralight looked like a giant stick insect, but it guided them to where Sam lay, his face shaded by his father's shadow, his skin white against his black hair.

'I was stupid, Sis!' he greeted Gaby, and she knelt and took his hand, the tears she'd held back for too long now raining down on his face.

Jack knelt beside her, reaching out for Sam's free wrist and frowning as he counted silently. Then he lifted the pale eyelids and peered into the dark eyes.

'Can you remember what happened?' he asked. 'Remember everything, or are there blank spaces?'

'I think I must have knocked myself out, because I remember waking up and wondering why I was lying on the ground. Then I tried to move, and my leg hurt, and I realised the bike was on top of me, and I could smell burning.'

Gaby saw the scorch mark on his jeans where the bike exhaust had started to burn into the thick material. She looked at her father, a shudder running through her as she saw her concern mirrored in his eyes.

'Can you move your fingers and toes?' Jack asked, and received a confirmatory nod that was followed immediately by a wince.

'Head hurt?'

'A bit,' Sam admitted, his strained voice revealing the lie behind the casual admission.

'I'm going to feel your head, then your neck, and then your leg,' Jack told him. 'I won't want bravery, but a good yell when anything I touch hurts. It's the only way we'll get some indication of the damage.'

He reached out and lifted Sam's head from the ground, his fingers moving against the skull with a delicate precision. Sam obliged with one yelp of pain, and Jack nodded.

'You'll need X-rays and should really have a scan. There's a big egg there but I don't think you've cracked your skull.' He looked up at James and added, 'There's no depressed fracture, which is good.'

He continued his examination, and Gaby watched, enthralled by the certainty in his movements, the tender thoroughness with which he tested Sam's body. As he felt the twisted leg, there was one gasp, then Sam fainted, and Jack moved more swiftly.

'I'd say it's a simple fracture and the bones haven't punctured the skin, but he'll have to go to hospital for X-rays and have it properly set.' He turned to Gaby. 'Does your service work on Christmas Day?'

She nodded, her heart hammering so hard in her chest that she wondered if she would ever be able to speak agian.

'I'll splint this as best I can and try to put some traction round his foot to keep the ends of the bone from rubbing together. Gaby, you find two straight sticks about this long——' he held out his hands for a moment. '—and, James, you might get on to the flying doctor, however you do that, and tell them he's got some concussion, possible skull fracture and a closed fracture of the femur. They will need to bring a proper traction splint.'

'I'll get the blanket and towels we carry in the back of the Land Rover, help you lift him then fly home and phone them.'

Her father sounded as relieved to have Jack there as she was, Gaby decided as she scouted around to find the sticks he would need to immobilise Sam's leg.

'Gaby will get the gear. If you're flying home, you might go now,' Jack suggested. 'When you get on to a doctor ask him if I can give him some morphine, if you have it in your medical chest, to dull the pain. If he says yes, bring it back here and I'll administer it before we move him. It would make the trip back to the house a lot more comfortable for him.'

James nodded, motioned to Gaby to take his place shading Sam's face, then hurried off to his new flying machine. As it lifted into the air, Gaby watched it apprehensively.

'There's so much potential for accidents with all these new-fangled inventions,' she said bitterly.

'And did no one ever fall off a horse or get trampled by cattle during a stampede before these new machines were put to use in the country?'

Jack continued to pad Sam's leg as he asked the question, and she watched the concentration with which he worked, visible even in the back of his head.

'Of course they did,' she sighed, shifting so that she could lift Sam's head into her lap. She wiped the dust away with her fingers, licking them and pressing them against the graze that seeped sluggishly on one downy cheek.

'I'm OK, Sis,' Sam whispered, then closed his eyes again.

'He is, Gaby!' Jack told her, repeating the assurance as he sat back on his heels and admired his handiwork.

They waited in silence as the sun grew hotter and hotter and flies gathered to torment them.

'Get the towels and blanket. I'll try to get him settled on that and use whatever we've got to immobilise the leg before your father gets back.'

As Gaby lifted Sam's head, to ease her leg out from under it, Jack stripped off his shirt and rolled it up, handing it to her to use as a makeshift pillow.

The movement seemed to disturb Sam. His eyes opened suddenly and he frowned up at the two watchers.

'I didn't shut the gate, Gaby,' he said, moving agitatedly, as if to get up so that he could go back to do it.

'It was shut when we came through,' Gaby told him, soothing him with light fingers on his hair.

'Not that gate,' he said crossly. 'The East Creek gate! I came that way and left it open, intending to go up as far as the old bore then back the same way.'

'I'll close it for you shortly, Scrappy,' she told him, but he wouldn't be humoured.

'There are cattle in the top paddock. I shouldn't have left it open at all! If some get into here they could be shut off without water. You've to to close it now.'

Gaby looked upwards, searching for a sign that her

father was returning. The blue sky remained empty and she turned to Jack.

'I'll have to ride his bike back anyway,' she said, trying to apologise for landing him in the midst of this family drama then deserting him. 'I might as well go now, to keep him happy.'

She smiled down at her brother who was still moving fretfully.

'If any cattle have come in, I'll herd them right back out again. I was doing it before you could walk, remember!'

'Get the towels and blanket first,' Jack reminded her. 'I'll make him comfortable while I wait for your father.' He looked at her in silence for a moment. 'Be careful, Gaby!' he added, his voice so full of unspoken thoughts that she was held immobile by it for a moment.

'I will,' she promised him, then hurried back to the vehicle for the things he needed. She bent and kissed Sam on the cheek before she moved away. Every fibre of her being wanted to press a similar salute on Jack's cheek, but the thought of reawakening Sam's concern kept her still.

She walked across to where her father had propped the bike, grimacing as she imagined that her white linen outfit was going to look like by the time she arrived home.

She heard the Ultra-light return as she followed the fence-line down towards the East Creek gate, then she saw the cattle which had moved through into the Old Bore paddock in search of fresh feed.

Would her father fly back this way and give her a hand? she wondered, circling them warily on the bike. The secret was not to hurry them, especially in the middle of the day, she reminded herself. She just had to go back and forth in front of them until they turned quietly and one decided to lead the others back out again.

It took over an hour to persuade them that they had to leave, and she yanked the gate shut and latched it with relief. Five minutes later, the bike spluttered to a halt.

Muttering wild oaths and even wilder revenge, she pushed it towards the house, wondering how long it would be before someone realised she was missing and sent out a search party for her.

The RFDS plane came in when she was still a mile from home, and she realised that her father and Jack would have driven Sam straight to the airstrip to meet it. She watched it lift into the air as she reached the doors of the machinery shed, and saw the waggle of its wings as it saluted the homestead.

Now the Land Rover was heading back up the track towards her, and she looked down at her grubby, dust-stained clothes and oil-smeared hands and legs.

Damn Scrappy, she thought, wishing that the ground would open up and swallow her her whole before Jack saw her looking like this—again!

But it was Bob, the senior stockman, who climbed out of the cabin of the Land Rover.

'Now the drama's over for the day, maybe we can have our Christmas dinner!' he said. His quick assessing glance took in her filthy state and simmering temper. 'After you've had a wash,' he added, grinning at her so cheerfully that she wanted to hit him.

CHAPTER TEN

IT WAS only natural that her father had flown to Derby with Sam, Gaby told herself, fixing a smile on to her face and pretending to enjoy her Christmas dinner. One parent would have to be with him for companionship as well as to give consent to any medical procedures that might be necessary, or to decide whether he should be flown on to Perth for specialist treatment.

And if only one parent was going, it would have had to be her father, since he refused to let her mother travel alone!

She praised Nell's cooking, and smiled as she passed the vegetable dish around the men, offering second helpings. But the feeling of having been cheated churned inside her. There had been *no* reason whatsoever for Jack to have accompanied Sam.

She had known as soon as she saw Bob in the Land Rover that Jack had walked out of her life again. He had said repeatedly that he shouldn't have come, so the moment an opportunity to escape had occurred he had seized it!

The interminable meal dragged to an end. The men cleared the table and washed the dishes as Teralga tradition decreed, while the three women sat back and, supposedly, relaxed. Nell held her hands clenched tightly in her lap waiting for the explosive noise of breaking crockery. Gaby frowned over her thoughts, while her mother's soft voice murmured on about Sam and presents and what a pity it had happened at Christmas.

When the phone rang, it broke up the tableau. Listening to the rumble of her father's stentorian tones and her mother's murmured replies, Gaby pieced together enough of the conversation to feel relief that Sam was OK and his leg was being set at that moment.

'They both send their love!'

'I think I'll have a rest,' Gaby declared as her mother replaced the receiver and turned away from the phone. The softened look of love she had caught in her mother's eyes was too much for her to bear.

She hurried down the passage, but her mother followed.

'Jack left a note for you,' she said, pulling a small slip of paper from the pocket of her dress. 'I didn't want to give it to you in front of the others.'

'Great!' Gaby muttered bitterly. 'That's twice he's run away and left a note. Last time it said. "Thanks"; I wonder what great message he's managed to convey this time?'

She snatched the paper from her mother's fingers and unfolded it.

'I think it's best this way, Gaby,' he had written. 'I could not bear to see more of you knowing that it could not last.'

She sank down on the bed, crushing the note in fingers rigid with pain. Wrapping her arms around her aching body, she rocked back and forth until her mother came to sit beside her and slid an arm around her shoulders. Like a child she turned to her for comfort, burying her head against the slight body and sobbing out all her agony.

'Why does it have to hurt like this? How can I feel

this way when I've only known him a week? How can I bear to feel like this forever? What am I going to do, Mum?'

She felt her mother's hand, stroking at her hair, and breathed deeply as she tried to re-gather her control.

'You could go after him,' her mother said quietly. 'Let him know it doesn't matter to you,'

Gaby's head shot up and she looked at the woman who had given birth to her with shock and astonishment in her eyes.

'You're saying I should offer myself to him as his mistress? That it doesn't matter that he has a wife?' Gaby felt the devastation of betrayal as she looked at her mother with total bewilderment. 'Mum, you're the one who has always taught me that happiness can't be bought at the expense of someone else—and that marriage vows are sacred!'

Now her perplexity was mirrored in her mother's face.

'But he's not married, Gaby,' she said, shaking her head as if to clear it. 'He can't be! He would have said!'

'Of course he's married!' Gaby flung the words at her, standing up from the bed and striding across the room as if her mental turmoil needed some physical release. 'Why else do you think he couldn't stay? Why else do you think he kept telling me he wasn't free to love me, that he couldn't offer me only half a person? Even his note said he had to go because it couldn't last. He's got a wife, Mum!' She yelled the words, flinging her arms into the air in a gesture of despair. 'And I knew that all along. I saw the woman with him in Broome! I knew he couldn't be mine, so why does it hurt so much?'

She threw herself back on the bed as her unhappiness brought tears flooding from her eyes.

'No, you must be wrong!' her mother declared, so definitely that Gaby raised her head enough to look at her out of one reddened eye. 'He talked to me, Gaby, probably more than he did to your father—or even to you—because he sensed I would understand.'

Was this one of her mother's 'feeling' things? Gaby wondered, but curiosity prompted her to mop her eyes and shuffle up to a sitting position on the bed.

'He feels betrayed by his body,' the older woman explained. 'Betrayed and vulnerable!' Her dark eyes, so like Gaby's own, pleaded for understanding. 'When the drop attacks, or whatever you like to call them, first started, he thought it was a sympton of something that could be diagnosed, then cured. He's a doctor, Gaby. He had to have faith in his own profession to set things right.'

'And they couldn't?'

'Not so far! In spite of a million tests, he says, they haven't found anything that might explain what is happening and why.'

Gaby nodded.

'He'd more or less told me that,' she said, a hint of the impatience she was feeling coming through the words. 'I suppose you talked to him about epilepsy?'

'Of course I did. He's had brain scans and EEG's and all the usual tests, but when the attacks kept persisting, and no one had found anything, he decided he'd try a different tack, and headed as far away as he could, as fast as he could——'

'With a blonde called Lauren!' Gaby interjected.

Her mother shook her head.

'No, you're wrong there, and I'm certain you're also

wrong about him being married. I know that Lauren followed him out here later, and if they are married why didn't she stay to spend Christmas with him?'

'But if he's not married why has he run away from me? Why does he keep saying that whatever it is between us can go no further? It must be a commitment to someone else! He loves me, Mum, I know he does, yet he says it can't go any further!'

Gaby's despair echoed round the room, filling all the little crevices with her grief.

'He says he doesn't want it to go further because he doesn't think it's fair to offer you a half-person.' The bitterness in the words hit Gaby like a sharp slap.

'He has drop attacks, Mum, and only occasional ones at that!' she protested. 'Why would that make him any less of a person? Why should it deny him a normal life with love included in it? No one's perfect, yet, somehow, people still manage to get married and have children and live a full life with their imperfections. Is Dr High and Mighty Fletcher too arrogant to accept that?'

'I understand how he feels!'

Her mother's simple statement interrupted the tirade, and Gaby stared at her.

'What do you mean?' she demanded, and saw her mother's head drop to shield her face from Gaby's probing eyes.'

'I feel I've let your father down with my epilepsy. Saddled him and you children with a burden you shouldn't have to bear.'

'That's ridiculous, Mum!' Gaby exploded. 'Utter rubbish!'

'I knew you would say that,' her mother replied,

'and your father would say the same thing, but I can't help feeling what I feel.'

She paused and the silence filled the room like a cold draught. Gaby remembered the disappointment on her mother's face when her father had spoken against an operation.

'And I can only guess that it's what Jack feels as well!' her mother added, cutting off any further protest from Gaby who was busy trying to work out this new angle to the problem.

'But. . .'

The word fluttered for a moment then died on her lips.

'I'll ring the hospital,' she announced. 'I'll ring and ask him.'

Her fingers were shaking so much that she wondered if she would ever get the number right, but after three attempts she heard the ringing tone, and the cheerful voice of one of the nursing staff.

'No, he's not here, Gaby! Your father came in with Sam. He's here. Shall I put him on?'

'Please!'

'Jack left us at the airport, love. Reckoned Sam was in good hands, said he'd better be getting on with some kind of life, and that was that. Jed Roberts was flying someone to Broome, and he hitched a lift with him that far.'

Gaby stared at the phone in disbelief, then said goodbye to her father and hung up, her fingers already fumbling through the phone book to find the number of the Cable Beach Club.

'But he was there last week,' she argued with the receptionist when she got through. 'He's heading back to Broome today; he's sure to want a room there again.'

'He must have changed his mind,' the woman replied. 'We had a call from him in Derby only an hour or so ago. We'd been holding his luggage here, and he asked for it to be sent to Broome Airport. I got the impression he was catching this afternoon's flight to Perth.'

Gaby dropped the receiver, panic catching at her throat and hammering at her agitated heart. He was getting further and further away from her—and all because, if her mother was right, he had some bizarre idea that his illness—whatever it was—would make him unacceptable to her!

'He's catching this afternoon's flight to Perth,' she told her mother with bleak resignation.

'It doesn't leave for another two and a half hours,' her mother said, glancing down at the slim gold watch she always wore.

A lightness skipped through Gaby—a possibility—some hope!

'You're right, Mum. I'll go to Broome!' she announced, then added as if excusing her sudden decision, 'Dad will have to get back here somehow. I'll ring him from Broome to let him know I'm there and will take him home, then ring you and tell you what's happening.'

Seizing an overnight bag, she threw some clothes into it, then rushed through the house, calling Bob from the kitchen to drive her down to the airstrip and help with fuel for the Piper.

The sky was bright and clear, and the air cooler at four thousand feet, but the old familiar joy of flying had been replaced by trepidation. As every minute passed, she grew closer to her goal, but uncertainty dogged her.

Broome Airport gave her clearance to land—half an hour before the southern flight was due in.

Was half an hour long enough to say all that she had to say?

It was long enough to find out if he was married! she reminded herself, trying to calm the agitation she was feeling.

She left her bag in the plane and raced towards the passenger terminal. He emerged from the building when she was still twenty yards away, his arms stretched wide and a frown of concern on his face. Had he recognised the Piper, or simply seen a mad woman running around in one hundred-and-four-degree heat and decided it had to be her?

'What's happened, Gaby?' he asked as he caught her and held her close. 'Is it Sam? Your mother? What's up?'

She looked up into his face and saw the tension and strain that battled the love in his eyes.

'Are you married to Lauren?' she demanded as he ushered her out of the blinding sun and searing heat, through the door into the cool air-conditioned building.

Their progress halted abruptly—on the pad that kept the automatic doors open!

'Of course not!' he replied, frowning down at her. 'Why ever would you think that?'

'Because you kept on telling me you weren't free, stupid!' she stormed. 'Because you kept saying whatever it was between us couldn't last. That you couldn't offer me half a man! What else was I supposed to think?'

As she looked up at the handsome face, she saw it tighten, and wanted to stamp her foot.

'And don't give me all that rot about having something wrong with you!' she yelled, then looked around at the appreciative audience that was gathering to watch her tantrum.

'Come in here!'

She grabbed his hand and dragged him towards the manager's small office.

'I need your room, Ted,' she said, jerking her head towards the door.

'But——' A bemused manager opened his mouth to protest, but the words were quickly swallowed when Gaby glared at him and jerked her head again.

Out! Immediately! she was saying, silently, and he smiled half-heartedly then left.

'Now!' Gaby announced, propping herself against Ted's desk for support and frowning up at the man who had stolen her heart. 'Perhaps you'd like to explain why you keep running away from me? Perhaps you'd like to tell me what terrible secret must keep us apart, if you're not married to the blonde bombshell?'

Jack shook his head, the colour fading from his skin as if inner tensions were draining the blood from his body.

'Gaby. . .' he began, softly, hesitantly—apologetically! He spread his hand apart and looked at her with mute appeal, but she was not going to give in. However feeble his excuse for running away from her, she intended to hear it, and hear it from him.

She folded her arms across her chest and waited—implacable.

'I told you about the fainting spells.' His voice pleaded for her understanding. 'I told you that I've had

every imaginable test but none of them proved
conclusive.'

'So?' she prompted.

'I suppose if I knew what was wrong with me, if I
knew it could be treated, or controlled even if it
couldn't be cured, I might feel differently. . .'

Again his voice died away, as if the silly physical
imperfection were a problem too embarrassing to contemplate—let alone discuss.

'Look at you,' he muttered. 'Young and radiant, so
beautiful you take my breath away. What right have I
to saddle you with an old crock? How could I even
consider letting you take on someone who might have
a progressive, debilitating illness of some kind? What
kind of love would it be, that gave you nothing but
pain?'

Her mother had been right! This stupid man kept
walking away from her because of some misguided idea
of chivalry or fair play or something.

She flung out her arms in disbelief, sending a tin of
pens flying across Ted's desk, knocking into things and
spilling everywhere.

'I can't believe this!' she stormed. 'I can't believe
you think you have the right to make judgements about
what might or might not be good for me! Or that you're
so full of self-pity that you would even think I'd turn
away from you because you're ill, or not want you
because, in your own eyes, you're less than perfect.'

She paused for breath, conscious of a stirring among
the group of people beyond the windows of Ted's
office. Was the plane coming in? How much time did
she have?

Jack Fletcher was studying the floor, and his bowed
head made her even angrier!

'Do you think love can be turned on or off because of circumstances? Do you think a parent, told her child has leukaemia, can love that child less because its dying, can say, I don't want this one any more, I'll have another, thanks?' Do you think there's any love without pain, without concern for each other, without risks and heartaches?'

Still he studied the floor, and her anger grew and grew until she was flinging words at him in a tumbling incoherent fury.

'What sort of guarantee are you looking for? One week, a month, a year, five years? What if I'm killed in a plane crash next week? Will it be any easier to bear because you haven't let yourself love me? Haven't shown me the ultimate joys of love, the sharing and caring and total togetherness that we both know could exist between us?'

There was a faint cheer from outside, and she looked distractedly towards the windows to see if she could see the southern plane.

Most of the people in the terminal building seemed to be looking upwards rather than outwards, but she knew that time was running out, and still this man refused to budge from his stubborn, head-bent contemplation of the floor.

'I love you, Jack,' she said desperately. 'Doesn't that mean anything to you? I love *you*—not a health certificate! Not some perfect physical specimen with no flaws or faults or weaknesses. We all have those! Who knows what might be wrong with me? It's like the dogs at home, Jack. As they get older they can no longer do the work they used to do, but we don't take them out and shoot them because they can't work. We don't love them any less because they've got old and smelly.'

As another cheer erupted from outside, she saw him raise his head. His eyes met hers, so full of love that she felt quick sick, then she saw the rueful smile that stretched his lips, and hope stirred within her.

'Not smelly, Gaby,' he protested, reaching out to take her in his arms. 'If I got smelly, I definitely want to be taken out and shot.'

As his lips met hers, she relaxed against him, almost sobbing in relief. A roar of engines outside told her the southern flight had arrived. Ted pushed through the door, chuckling to himself, while the crowd beyond him in the waiting-room cheered and hooted.

'You've just proposed to that man over the loud-speakers, Gaby,' he told her, waving his hand towards the uproarious crowd. 'And now that you seem to have reached a satisfactory conclusion, I would like my office back so I can get this plane safely on its way back to Perth.'

Gaby felt the blush start at her toes, and she buried her head in Jack's shoulder to hide her flaming cheeks.

'There's so much we have to talk about, and so little time,' Jack whispered against her hair. 'I know what you're saying, Gaby, and I love you more because of it—if that's possible—but there are practical aspects. There are possibilities that must be discussed. Love might seem enough, but stresses can destroy the strongest love if they're not dealt with sensibly.'

'We'll talk,' Gaby promised. 'Come back with me to Teralga or to Derby—my flat there. We'll be on our own,' she whispered, blushing again but for a different reason.

'I'm booked on this flight to Perth,' he objected, but once again she heard the words he wasn't saying.

I love you, love you, love you, rang in her head, blotting out everything else.

'I want to see some people, talk about some things.'

She pulled away from him and frowned up into his face.

'More tests!' she accused. 'I don't care about your health—well, I do care about it, but not in any way that would affect our relationship,' she mumbled as, watching him smile, her knees went weak.

'You'd better decide if you're going on this flight or not,' Ted interrupted. 'Passengers are all off and we'll start embarkation in ten minutes.'

'I'm going,' Jack said, the words merging with Gaby's definite,

'He's staying.'

'I have to go, but not for the reasons you think,' he whispered to her, bending to kiss her lips again. 'I want to see people from your medical association about registration here, and speak to someone I know who's at the university in Perth. Maybe lecturing would be a possibility.'

Gaby clung to him, unable to reconcile his determination to go with the words of love he'd uttered. One arm held her close against his chest, while his free hand fished in his pocket.

'Look, Gaby,' he said softly. 'Look at this.'

He handed her his plane ticket and for a moment she stared blankly at it. Then she opened it up.

'It's a return ticket,' she whispered, her heart fluttering in her throat as she looked up and caught the love his eyes were beaming down on her. 'You were coming back?'

'I had to, Gaby,' he said softly. 'The further we flew from Teralga, the more certain I was that I was doing the wrong thing. By the time I reached Derby I knew that, somehow, I had to make a new life for myself that I might possibly be able to share with you. I didn't know whether you would want to share it. And I knew I was selfish to want you with me, but I also knew I had to ask you.'

'I'm about to call all passengers on to that flight,' Ted warned.

'The sooner I get things sorted out in Perth, the sooner I can get back to you, Gaby,' Jack murmured, but her arms crept around his body and she clung, limpet-like, to him.

'It's Christmas Day! No one will want to see you until after New Year. I'd come with you, but I can't leave Mum on her own at Teralga worrying about Sam. Come back with me, and I'll fly you down to Perth in the new year.'

'You'll be back at work,' he protested, but his arms were now around her body, and he held her as if he would never let her go.

'I'll take some leave—even flying-doctor pilots get holidays, you know!'

'Last call!' Ted said, but they did not hear him, too intent on tasting again the magic of their kisses and the uniqueness of their love.

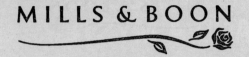

MILLS & BOON

LOVE CALL

The books for enjoyment this month are:

NEVER SAY NEVER	Margaret Barker
DANGEROUS PHYSICIAN	Marion Lennox
THE CALL OF DUTY	Jessica Matthews
FLIGHT INTO LOVE	Meredith Webber

——————— 🍎 ———————

Treats in store!

Watch next month for the following absorbing stories:

A FAMILIAR STRANGER	Caroline Anderson
ENCHANTING SURGEON	Marion Lennox
DOWNLAND CLINIC	Margaret O'Neill
A MATTER OF ETHICS	Patricia Robertson

Available from W.H. Smith, John Menzies, Forbuoys, Martins, Tesco, Asda, Safeway and other paperback stockists.

Readers in South Africa - write to:
IBS, Private Bag X3010, Randburg 2125.

GET 4 BOOKS
AND A MYSTERY GIFT

Return this coupon and we'll send you 4 Love on Call novels and a mystery gift absolutely FREE! We'll even pay the postage and packing for you.

We're making you this offer to introduce you to the benefits of Reader Service: FREE home delivery of brand-new Love on Call novels, at least a month before they are available in the shops, FREE gifts and a monthly Newsletter packed with information.

Accepting these FREE books and gift places you under no obligation to buy, you may cancel at any time, even after receiving just your free shipment. Simply complete the coupon below and send it to:

MILLS & BOON READER SERVICE, FREEPOST, CROYDON, SURREY, CR9 3WZ.

No stamp needed

Yes, please send me 4 free Love on Call novels and a mystery gift. I understand that unless you hear from me, I will receive 4 superb new titles every month for just £1.99* each postage and packing free. I am under no obligation to purchase any books and I may cancel or suspend my subscription at any time, but the free books and gifts will be mine to keep in any case. (I am over 18 years of age)

2EP5D

Ms/Mrs/Miss/Mr _____

Address _____

_____

_____ Postcode _____

MILLS & BOON

Betty Neels

Bestselling romances brought back to you by popular demand

Two complete novels in one volume
by bestselling author

Betty Neels

The Convenient Wife
Roses Have Thorns

Available: October 1995   Price: £3.99